"How did you ever manage this alone?"

Kyra soaped one triplet's back and arms and dodged a splash from another. He chortled and splashed again.

"My cousin helped out," Wade said. "Sometimes. Once we get them in the tub, the rest is cake."

The little girl grabbed for her brother's favorite ducky, who then boo-hooed.

Wade rescued the situation, all the while singing, "Rub-a-dub-dub, three kids in a tub."

"Cake for you," Kyra said, bumping his side. "Rock-hard biscuits for me."

Wade's head turned. Twinkling blue eyes were so close she could see the yellow sunbursts around his pupils. "I didn't want to say anything."

"Kind of obvious, wasn't it?" She smiled into those eyes.

He smiled back.

She heard a kerplunk from somewhere.

Hopefully, not from her heart.

Linda Goodnight, a *New York Times* bestselling author and winner of a RITA® Award in inspirational fiction, has appeared on the Christian bestseller list. Her novels have been translated into more than a dozen languages. Active in orphan ministry, Linda enjoys writing fiction that carries a message of hope in a sometimes dark world. She and her husband live in Oklahoma. Visit her website, lindagoodnight.com, for more information.

Books by Linda Goodnight

Love Inspired

Sundown Valley

To Protect His Children

The Buchanons

Cowboy Under the Mistletoe
The Christmas Family
Lone Star Dad
Lone Star Bachelor

Whisper Falls

Rancher's Refuge
Baby in His Arms
Sugarplum Homecoming
The Lawman's Honor

Visit the Author Profile page at Harlequin.com for more titles.

To Protect
His Children

Linda Goodnight

LOVE INSPIRED
INSPIRATIONAL ROMANCE

LOVE INSPIRED®
INSPIRATIONAL ROMANCE

PLEASE RECYCLE
THIS PRODUCT IS RECYCLABLE

Recycling programs
for this product may
not exist in your area.

ISBN-13: 978-1-335-48884-8

To Protect His Children

This edition published by arrangement with Harlequin Books S.A.

For questions and comments about the quality of this book, please contact us at CustomerService@Harlequin.com.

Love Inspired
22 Adelaide St. West, 40th Floor
Toronto, Ontario M5H 4E3, Canada
www.Harlequin.com

Printed in U.S.A.

I will lift up mine eyes unto the hills, from whence cometh my help. My help cometh from the Lord, which made heaven and earth.
—*Psalms* 121:1–2

For the glory of my Lord and Savior, Jesus. And in memory of my son, Travis. Someday I'll see you both. Won't that be a grand day?

Chapter One

Wade Trudeau was losing his mind. What was left of it, anyway.

He slammed the landline back on the charger, pressed the heels of his hands against his eyes and groaned.

"No news from the employment agency?"

Wade let his arms flop to the desktop and looked up as his cousin, best friend and business partner, Bowie Trudeau ambled into the home office of Sundown Ranch.

"The trouble is, Bowie, nobody wants to take on three babies, especially in an area as remote as Sundown Ranch."

"We're only ten miles from town."

"Might as well be a thousand the way these town folks behave." No woman, including their own mother, seemed willing to care for three little babies.

"We were making it work until Miss Janey's brother got sick."

Miss Janey, a diamond in a gray ponytail.

"I can't fault Janey for putting her brother first. That's what family does." Wade's mouth twisted at the irony. His own family wasn't so adoring. "Or what they *should* do. And the two other housekeeper/nannies barely got unpacked before they were packing up again."

"No calls from those index cards you posted in town?"

The little mountain town of Sundown Valley was friendly like that. People stuck ads for yard work, baby-sitting, hay-hauling and whatever on community bulletin boards in cafés and grocery stores. Even in the pink Laundromat.

Last year, with a simple index card and a phone number, Wade had given away a litter of abandoned kittens.

Babies abandoned by their mother, apparently, were a different matter.

"None." Depressive air descended like morning fog over Jackfork Mountain.

Wade heard a familiar babble. One of the babies was awake. If he didn't hurry, the fifteen-month-old would elevate to an ear-splitting pitch that would wake the entire trio.

He loped toward the nursery, then tiptoed into the triplets' bedroom to scoop up the pajama-clad baby and quickly escape to the hallway.

"Good morning, nugget," he whispered.

He should have known the babbler was Abby. She'd been trying to talk since she was born.

Abby burrowed her face into the space between his neck and shoulder, a spot where his babies fit perfectly.

Wade's chest filled with pleasure. This was his baby girl. His daughter. A gift from God. No matter how difficult the journey, he was grateful for his babies.

Wade breathed in Abby's sleep-warmed scent. The hint of last night's bath marathon lingered in her hair. He probably hadn't rinsed well enough, a real challenge with a slick, wiggling toddler and two more waiting in the wings.

He was still learning, still adjusting to being both mom and dad. Two cowboys plus three babies equaled chaos.

He patted Abby's tiny back and headed for the kitchen for a fruit pouch to keep her happy while he rustled up breakfast.

Bowie had disappeared already, probably heading out to meet the vet. As if they didn't have enough to worry about, some of the cows in pasture three were coughing and bull five had a limp.

As he settled Abby into one of the trio of highchairs crowding the kitchen island, the doorbell rang.

Wade looked toward the baby, then toward the ringing bell and let out a beleaguered mutter.

He knew better than to leave a baby alone in a highchair, even for a minute. He'd learned the hard way.

Quickly unbuckling the safety straps, he pulled Abby onto one hip. She wasn't happy.

He pushed the fruit pouch against her lips and hurried to the door.

Then wished he'd ignored it.

"Keno," he said, wary.

A red-faced Bud Keno shoved a piece of paper into Wade's gut. Wade grabbed for it.

"What's this?"

"A bill for the four calves I didn't get out of my bull."

"How's that my fault?"

"Your bull busted through my fence, and now I got four calves that don't fit my breeding program."

Was that why bull five was limping? He'd been battling Keno's bulls? "If you'd keep your side of the fences repaired—"

Keno stuck a finger against Wade's nose. "Eight thousand or I'm suing."

While Wade tried to regain his breath and hold his temper, Keno marched to his truck and sped away.

Wade crumpled the bill in one hand.

"Starting out to be a real bad day." He sniffed at the baby. "And now, you stink."

He managed to change the dirty diaper before the next interruption.

The doorbell. Again.

"Lord," he said to the ceiling, "if that's Keno again I may have to act first and ask forgiveness afterward."

Storming through the house with his daughter on his hip and growing madder by the minute, Wade reached the door and yanked it open.

"What now?" he bellowed.

A startled young woman took two steps backward. "Have I come at a bad time?"

Was there anything other than a bad time lately?

"Sorry. It's been a rough morning." As if to prove his point, Abby slapped him upside the head with the fruit pouch. He felt a dribble down the side of his face and swiped a hand over it.

Nothing like first impressions.

"I'm looking for Wade Trudeau."

"That's me."

"I'm Kyra Mason." Eyes still wide and uncertain, she pointed. "You have a baby?"

He scowled. "You don't like kids."

She stiffened. "Of course I do. Everyone likes children."

His mouth twisted. "Apparently not."

Abby patted his whiskered face. So he hadn't shaved yet today. No wonder the woman—Kyra Mason—stared at him with something akin to suspicion. He probably looked like America's Most Wanted.

Had he even combed his hair this morning?

Wade glanced from the woman's wary hazel eyes to the driveway and the tiniest blue car he'd ever seen. Was she a…salesman, er, woman? "Is there something I can do for you?"

She hitched a large shoulder bag and handed him a familiar white index card. He recognized his own handwriting.

Oh.

Well, now.

This could be promising. Maybe his lousy day was taking a turn for the better.

Thank you, Lord. Please let her be the one. You know I'm sinking fast.

He'd prayed over this nanny situation at least a hundred times. Maybe God was finally showing him some mercy. Except Kyra Mason looked nothing like the sixty-year-old grandmother he had in mind.

After a quick glance at Keno's bill, now crumbled on the entry tile, Wade put on his nice face. If Kyra Mason was here about the nanny job, he didn't want to scare her to death.

"You're applying for the position?"

Her eyes went to the baby. "Maybe."

Wade bit back a growl. What was it with women these days? Weren't they supposed to be baby-adoring nurturers? Or was that only a TV fantasy created by a wishful-thinking male?

This woman said she liked kids, but the uncertainty in her expression made him wonder.

He wasn't sure he could take much more rejection, especially when it came to his triplets.

But he'd invite her in and ask. He was that desperate.

Stepping back from the door opening, he hitched his chin. "Office is the first room on the right. Come in."

He waited until she passed, then shut the front door and followed her into the ranch office.

The smell of her perfume trailed behind her, and Wade called himself seven kinds of idiot because he liked it. A woman's perfume was a dangerous thing.

Giving his head a shake as a reminder of what the last woman and her delicious perfume had done to him and their babies, he settled behind his desk with Abby on his lap.

Kyra chose one of the beige armchairs across from

him. She let her purse slide from her shoulder to the floor, placed a manila file folder on her lap, sat up fence-post straight and clenched her hands atop the folder.

She was either nervous or a prissy little prig, her posture perfect, her lips tight, her nose tilted up just so. Granted, hers was a cute nose. So was the rest of her face. Not Hollywood gorgeous but fresh and wholesome, like a spring morning.

Perfectly groomed in an interview-worthy floral dress and sensible black shoes, she had smooth shoulder-length red hair, the kind that caught sunbeams.

Yeah, so he'd noticed the shiny stuff on some subconscious male level while he'd barked at her on the front porch.

She was pretty, but he wasn't looking for beauty. He'd had that. He wanted a woman willing to nurture his babies while he worked. Period. End of subject. Cut. Print. The end.

"Tell me about yourself, Kyra." There. Didn't he sound businesslike?

The redhead whipped out a printed parchment résumé and placed it in his outstretched hand. Their fingers touched. Only a brush of skin, and then she sat back, but not before Wade's nerve endings reacted. His hands were hard and calloused. Hers were as soft as Abby's.

Dropping the résumé on the desk as if it had suddenly burst into flames, he slid his hand beneath the desk and scraped his fingertips across the rough denim of his jeans. Rough. Not soft. Much better.

Abby made a dive for the pristine white paper. Reflexes always on the ready, especially since becoming the only parent of three babies, Wade rescued the résumé from her grip and slid the wiggling child to the floor.

She toddled off to explore. The house was babyproofed but he kept an eye on her anyway.

Babies, in his crash course of experience, had an uncanny way of finding things they shouldn't no matter how a man tried. One person didn't have enough hands or eyes. How mothers managed still mystified him.

He perused the slightly wrinkled résumé. "You're a teacher."

His eyebrows lifted in surprise.

"I was. I'm considering a change."

"Teacher burnout already?" He softened the question with a slight smile. At least, he hoped it was a smile and not a grimace.

Kyra didn't return his feeble attempt. Instead, her lips formed a tight line, as if she didn't want to discuss the subject. "Something like that."

Okay, fair enough. He wouldn't pry. From the news and teacher friends, he had an idea of the pressures of dealing with twenty-five-plus kids in an enclosed space, half of those students without any home training. Teachers were leaving the profession in a stampede.

Still, a teaching education and her experience working with kids would be valuable when caring for toddlers. "Can you pass a drug test?"

She whipped out two more papers from her handy little folder. So organized.

"Most recent drug test and a background check. Standard procedure for educators." She pushed her folder across his desk. "References in there, too. I can get more if needed."

While he read the glowing references, Abby toddled toward the newcomer, chattering with every wobbly step. She patted the woman on the knee, smearing a dab of applesauce on the blue floral dress.

Wade watched from the corner of one eye. Kyra didn't react to the smudge, a major point in her favor. Babies were messy. Sticky. Smelly. Noisy.

He cast an ear toward the nursery. Why weren't the boys up? Not that he was complaining.

Abby reached up with chubby arms. As natural as could be, Kyra Mason lifted his baby girl against her shoulder for a messy hug. If the former teacher even noticed the smears and dribbles of pureed fruit soiling her nice clothes, she ignored them.

What kind of woman did that?

Wade clapped the folder shut. "Looks good to me. When can you start?"

To say she was startled by Wade Trudeau's sudden decision was a massive understatement. Kyra batted her eyes so many times in an attempt to get her bearings she lost focus.

"Wait. Wait. Mr. Trudeau."

"Wade."

"Right. Yes. Okay. Wade." She was stuttering. But she hadn't expected an immediate job offer. "I'm not sure yet if I *want* the position."

The handsome cowboy fell back in his chair. His voice became a despairing murmur. "Is it because of the applesauce?"

"What? Applesauce?" She followed his gaze to her sleeve. "I was a special needs teacher. I've had far worse things on my clothes than pureed fruit."

The cowboy tilted his head back against his office chair and closed his eyes for one long breath.

For a second, Kyra felt sorry for him. He looked tired. Frazzled. Beneath the uncombed brown hair and whiskery face, he was a good-looking cowboy, in a rugged Scott Eastwood kind of way.

The sleeves of his blue chambray shirt were rolled to the elbows over muscular forearms. Strong hands. Muscled chest. Broad shoulders.

Did ranch work keep all cowboys in such great shape? Heat rose up the back of her neck.

This was a job interview, not a speed date.

To hide her foolish thoughts, she pressed her face against the baby's neck. She smelled like baby shampoo.

"Then what's the holdup?" he asked. "The job's open now. Today. I can pay you well." He named a satisfactory, though surprising sum, considering the nature of the job.

Which begged the question.

What exactly was she required to do to earn that amount of money?

"Stay long enough and I'll even put you on our medical."

"Mr. Trudeau. Wade. We haven't even discussed a job description. Your card said housekeeper. What exactly does this housekeeping position entail?"

"Well, uh—" He ran a finger beneath his shirt collar, a weird action because the top button was open on the casual shirt. "I might have left off the nanny part."

"*Nanny* part?"

This was supposed to be a job *without* children. In fact, bearing the responsibility of a child was the very thing she'd hoped to avoid.

Besides, what kind of parent hired a stranger on the spot to care for his child without even calling references?

Her opinion of the handsome cowboy, already questionable, hit rock bottom.

An hour ago, she'd driven away from a school parking lot too anxious to go inside to the scheduled interview for a teaching position. She'd thought she was ready to teach again. The cold sweats and shaky hands proved she wasn't.

At a coffee shop in the sleepy town of Sundown Valley, she'd seen Wade Trudeau's index card on a bulletin board advertising for a housekeeper at the Sundown Ranch. No mention of a child at all. On an impulse she still didn't understand other than her love for the Kiamichi Mountain area, Kyra had taken the card and driven to the ranch.

She needed a job. But did she want one with a child involved?

"Your card didn't mention a baby."

"Three." He held up three fingers, spearing her with a pair of tired blue eyes as if awaiting her reaction.

"Three what?"

"Babies."

Shock reverberated down Kyra's spine. *Three* babies? As in triplets?

She picked her chin up off the floor to consider exactly what she'd walked into.

Nanny to three children.

"Not a housekeeping job at all?" Had her voice squeaked a tad on the ending?

"Light housekeeping. We pick up after ourselves, but the triplets don't. Maybe a little cooking if you're willing, but if not, Bowie and I will go on handling KP duties."

"Who's Bowie?" She was starting to sound like a five-year-old, answering every statement with a question. But really, this man was so rattled, he was confusing her.

"Didn't I mention him? My cousin and business partner. He lives here, too."

Kyra raised her eyebrows. "Anyone else I should know about?"

And why didn't she put this cute baby down right now and head for the door? This obviously was not the job for her. Nothing, not one thing, was the way she'd imagined.

The cowboy's mouth gave a wry twist. "No one else at the moment. I have a wayward brother. Yates. But he hasn't been around in several years."

From the sad look in his eyes, the wayward brother

was an issue he had yet to resolve. She couldn't think about that. She had issues of her own.

"So you're telling me, two men live in this house, but no women."

"Right. Plus three fifteen-month-old babies. We need a nanny in the worst way."

"Do you actually expect a woman to move in here, miles from the nearest town, with two strange men?"

That silenced him. His shoulders slumped. The frown, which seemed permanent, deepened.

Finally, he muttered, "Is that why no one wants the job?"

"It could be one reason."

"Do I look scary to you?" He touched his unshaven face, then held up a hand stop-sign style. "Don't answer that."

Kyra almost laughed. The poor guy was beside himself.

"Have you considered alternative lodging for your nanny?"

"Alternative…" His fingers scraped over the whiskery jaw as he considered. "Well, let's see. We have an old bunkhouse around back, but the place hasn't been used in years."

"Separate living quarters, I think, would help in your nanny search."

"Will you take the job if I fix it up?"

"What about time off?"

He looked thunderstruck. "Babies don't take time off."

"I wonder if that's another reason you're having a hard time finding a caregiver? Everyone needs some free time."

"I'm a rancher. I don't even know what free time looks like. But if you'll take the job, pick your days. Any days. Ranch work doesn't care. It keeps going. Like babies."

He sat up straighter, seemingly bolstered by what he thought was a great offer, as if normal days off would turn the tide in his favor.

It wouldn't, though she felt sorry for the three babies whose daddy seemed so eager to escape them.

"To be honest," Kyra said, "a nanny position wasn't what I was expecting. I'll have to say no. I don't think I'm interested."

She didn't know why she'd come here in the first place.

She started to put Abby on the floor.

"Wait. Hear me out. I'll pay a bonus." Wade's voice rose in anguish.

He leaned those fit forearms on the desk and stretched his hands toward her.

A plea. A pitiable, desperate plea.

"Why not take the job on a trial basis?" he was saying. "Three months. Until the end of summer. Three short months of sunshine and mountain air and country peace and quiet. School is out for the summer, anyway. If you choose to return to teaching in September, so be it. I'll pay you the fat bonus, anyway."

"For only three months?" She could definitely use the money. And she loved the idea of mountain solitude.

He nodded, solemn as a gravedigger. "Three months gives me time to look for someone else. Not that I hold out much hope. I've been searching for months."

"Have you considered a male nanny?"

"I want a woman."

When she tilted her head, he added, "What I mean is, I don't want a woman *personally.*" He made a face. "Not ever. No thanks. The gain is not worth the pain."

He was certainly adamant. She'd be insulted for the entire female population if the man weren't desperately seeking a female nanny. "Then why not a male nanny?"

"Call me old-fashioned, but no. They have plenty of

men in their lives. I want a woman. The balance thing. God's design."

Kyra understood where he was coming from. In her studies and in her classroom, she'd noted the importance of both a female and a male in a child's life. Thus, the value of mentoring organizations like Big Brothers and Big Sisters.

That Wade Trudeau needed her was evident, and she'd always been a soft touch, especially where kids were involved.

She wanted to help the babies. She really did. But a ranch with two men and three toddlers was out of her comfort zone.

"Have you considered a day-care center rather than a nanny?"

"Yes and no." He made a growling noise and pulled a face. "I've considered a day care and weighed the pros and cons. The answer is still no. Too far away and too expensive. Don't you get it? I want the triplets here, with me."

The sincerity in his voice went straight to Kyra's heart. Maybe he wasn't the jerk she'd assessed him to be.

He had a ranch to run. Having the triplets on site, in his house, allowed him to pop in from time to time to see them.

Was that his intent? Or was she reading her own emotions into the situation?

Poor little babies.

If she stayed in this office another minute, she might seriously be tempted to say yes.

"Let's do this," Kyra said, in a pity move as she reached for her folder. The baby squirmed at the pressure. Kyra sat her on the floor and took a pen from her purse. "Give me three character references I can contact. I'll check them and call you with my answer sometime tomorrow."

Saying no was easier over the phone.

Suddenly, loud cries erupted from somewhere in the house. Extremely loud, angry, frustrated someone-save-me squalls.

Kyra's head snapped in that direction.

The other two babies, apparently, had awakened.

Should she offer assistance? Or get out while she had a chance?

Wade bolted to his feet. His chair clattered backward on its rollers. "I missed the signals."

"What?"

"The babies babble first. Screaming comes after they're tired of waiting for me."

He raked his hand over his head. Messy brown hair shot straight up.

Abby toddled to him. He bent to pick her up.

Kyra took pity on him.

"Go," Kyra said. "I've got her."

The poor guy galloped away like a juiced-up race-horse.

Chapter Two

When Wade returned with the freshly diapered boys, each calmed with a fruit pouch, he found Kyra Mason sitting on the floor in her pretty floral dress, rolling a wadded ball of paper back and forth to Abby.

In a warm singsong voice, she said, "Throw, catch. Throw, catch. What a smart girl you are!"

She clapped her hands. Abby took this as the signal for patty cake.

With a chuckle, Kyra played the game, ending with a belly tickle. Abby cackled.

At that moment, Wade decided he'd do anything in his power to convince Kyra to become his nanny.

He was willing to beg.

And raise her salary.

And turn the bunkhouse into a castle.

Even if he had to sell a bull or two.

"Looks like you and Abby hit it off." *Please say yes.*

He lowered the boys onto the floor.

"This is Benjamin." He touched Ben's soft brown hair. "That one is Caden."

"They look identical." She lightly patted each boy's chubby leg and rose from the floor, leaving Abby to play with a snow globe he kept on his desk for that very purpose.

"They are. Abby is my outlier. Fact was, we didn't know she was in there until their birthday."

"Quite the surprise."

"Shock's more like it." Followed by the most overwhelming joy and responsibility, plus a tidal wave of other emotions that nearly brought him to his knees. Still did at times.

He'd been prepared for two rough-and-tumble boys. A sweet pink girl, not so much. Though now he couldn't imagine life without her.

"They were pretty small and had to be in newborn NICU for a while, so I'd stand at the window counting them, praying for them."

He didn't know why he'd told her that.

Kyra trailed a hand over the top of Benjamin's dark cap of hair. The baby looked up and grinned.

"May I ask about their mother?"

Wade's insides went on the defensive. The dark cloud of fury rose, tornadic in proportions. "They don't have a mother."

His words were terse. Harsh.

Kyra's face pinkened. She settled her gaze on the triplets and avoided looking at him.

An uncomfortable tension stretched between them, vibrating like a rattlesnake. His fault. He'd scared her with his bitterness.

He tried to keep the anger to himself, but one unexpected mention of Sabrina and the rage roared in to attack the closest person. Poor Bowie had taken the brunt of his hostility for a long time. The subject of Sabrina was taboo.

"I should go." Kyra reached down for her purse.

Oh, no. He'd messed up big-time. She was leaving. "Wait. My references."

Her mouth opened and closed before she nodded. "Right."

From the looks of her, she had no intention of calling any of them.

She hitched her purse onto her shoulder and looked toward the door. Eager to escape.

He found his cell phone under a pile of contracts and scrolled for names and phone numbers of responsible souls who thought he was a good guy. He jotted three contacts on a notepad.

She accepted the note, saying nothing.

Panic pressed in. She was going to leave and never look back. She wouldn't call, probably wouldn't answer if he called her.

Three babies crowded around him, one hanging on to each jean leg, while the other, Benjamin, managed to find a piece of something to stick in his mouth.

Wade scooped him up. "Give it to Daddy, big guy."

Of course, Ben had no intention of relinquishing his treasure, so Wade pried the paper from his mouth and tossed it in the trash can.

"Look," he said, leaning his face around the now-screaming baby. "I'm sorry about barking at you. Twice. My ex-wife is a touchy subject."

"So I gathered. And none of my business." Kyra started out of the office.

Wiping baby slobber on his jeans, Wade followed.

He opened the door for her. She started off the porch. Wade wanted to say something other than *you smell good* or *please stay*, but was at a loss.

He'd blown his one chance at hiring a nanny.

Abby, clinging to his leg like a wood tick, turned loose and began to follow the redhead out the door. When Wade caught her tiny shoulder and turned her around, Abby started to cry, straining toward a woman she'd met less than an hour ago.

Wade knew how she felt.

He hoisted his daughter onto his other hip, blocked

Caden from tumbling out the door, while wrestling with the still-whining Ben who'd decided he wanted down.

In desperation, Wade yelled after the fleeing woman, "Three months, Kyra. That's all I'm asking. Three months."

Clearly, the man was desperate. He was also intense and cranky, even angry, though he undoubtedly loved his children. All three of them.

Triplets. My goodness.

Adorable, yes, but what a handful for any parent, especially a single man running a ranch far from town and a day care.

Kyra couldn't decide if she admired the guy for trying or thought he was a jerk with a bad attitude.

Either way, playing nanny to three babies, even for a summer, was more than she'd bargained for.

But she needed to work. Medical bills still flowed in like the Arkansas River, not to mention the money she wanted to send to Tristan's family.

Tristan. The very thought of the bright little boy with the mischievous grin made her heart bleed.

She drove to the end of the long graveled driveway leading in and out of the Sundown Ranch and stopped, debating.

Should she go home to her Tulsa suburb and forget this whole idea of finding peace and healing in the gorgeous southeastern Oklahoma mountains?

Or drive into the picturesque town of Sundown Valley and inquire about other employment opportunities?

She closed her eyes. "Heavenly Father, I thought You were leading me to this area. What now?"

Opening her eyes, she stared to the left and then the right, finally choosing the winding country road leading away from town and toward the low ancient mountains surrounding Sundown Valley.

Five minutes of driving took her along a scenic byway, the kind of place her family had visited every summer when she was a kid. She parked at an overlook and exited the car, taking her water bottle with her to the metal railing.

Drawing a deep breath, Kyra exhaled, the tension seeping from her body. She shook out her arms, stretched her fingers.

Not another car passed on the rural road. The only sound was occasional birdsong and the breeze whispering through the sumac shrubs at her feet.

"I need direction, Lord."

Staring across the vast valley of pine and hardwood to the undulating bluish mountains on the other side was a respite for the soul.

Across the way, she recognized the Winding Stair Mountains near where she and her parents had often rented a cabin or, in their more adventurous days, had pitched a tent.

"You do such glorious work, Father."

The breeze told her He was listening. She believed that with all her heart. In the year since the tragedy, she'd felt God's presence in these quiet moments when the pain subsided, both mental and physical.

"'I will lift up mine eyes unto the hills, from whence cometh my help. My help cometh from the Lord which made heaven and earth.'" As a pastor's daughter, she'd memorized many scriptures and this psalm of David seemed fitting. "I trust You, Lord. Guide me."

She lifted her finger and traced the winding road that curved like a long brown snake up the opposite mountain. Even after her mother died, she and her dad had hiked miles into the wilderness from that road.

She could return to the Tulsa area and find a job there easily enough. Everyone seemed to be hiring these days.

Yet, home brought memories she couldn't face and

people who were constant reminders. Everyone knew, and their well-meaning pity made things worse.

Three round innocent faces rose in her mind. Abby, Benjamin and Caden. ABC. Three precious babies with one very lost parent. Only one. *No mother*, he'd said, in a way that had made Kyra want to run.

Why would a woman leave her three babies? Was it the man? Was he such a difficult person that his wife had been compelled to escape? Why not take her beautiful children with her? Most mothers would. Wouldn't they?

Had Wade somehow wrestled custody from the triplets' mother?

Wade Trudeau and his triplets had left too many unanswered questions in her mind. She should have asked, but his overreaction had warned her off.

Why couldn't she get him and his babies out of her head?

Maybe because those babies needed her far more than the man did.

"Are You trying to tell me something, Lord?"

She sipped her bottled water, and then, taking out her cell phone, checked for a signal. Cell service was spotty in the Kiamichi.

"One bar." She might as well try calling Wade Trudeau's references. A single hint of negativity from anybody and her decision would be easy to make.

Ten minutes later, with the signal still holding, Kyra tapped her pastor-dad's photo.

The phone clicked.

"How'd the interview at Sundown Valley Elementary go?" That was Dad. Cut to the chase.

She pressed the speaker button and held the device below her chin. There was no one within miles to overhear. "I backed out."

"You didn't go to the interview?"

"I canceled."

Her dad, the Reverend Jack Mason, was silent for a few seconds. Kyra imagined the slight pull of his blond eyebrows as he pondered her words and the deeper meaning behind a canceled interview.

"Are you okay?" he asked.

Sweet dad. Unlike her, he was more concerned about her well-being than the fact that she hadn't worked in over a year.

"I am, but I'm not ready to teach again. I want to be, Dad, but I can't. I sat in the school parking lot for fifteen minutes trying to convince myself that the building was safe, that I could do this and that nothing terrible would happen."

"PTSD is a strange malady."

"When I realized I was shaky and in a cold sweat, I knew I couldn't go inside. I was on the verge of losing control."

She hadn't expected her triggers to follow her here, but the idea of stepping back into a classroom of kids overwhelmed her at the rural Sundown Valley school every bit as much as it had in the city.

She shuddered at the thought of experiencing a flashback in front of strangers during an interview.

"I'm sorry, Kyra. I'd hoped a change of location was the answer."

"So had I, but apparently any school building triggers the anxiety."

"So you're driving back home today?"

Home for most of the last year had been her father's spare bedroom in a suburb outside of Tulsa, the room she'd called her own as a child.

Dad had driven her to physical therapy, counseled her, cooked for her, prayed for her. All the things a loving parent should do for a broken, wounded child.

Now her body was healed. It was time to let her dad get back to his own very busy life.

"Actually, Dad, I'm considering another position down here."

"Something other than teaching?"

In the background of their call, she heard a door open and close, heard voices. A large church was a busy place, even during the week.

Was she really thinking of moving to a remote Kiamichi Mountain ranch for three months to care for a set of triplets? Seriously?

She glanced down into the lush green valley below.

Maybe she was.

"The job is a nanny position, Dad. At a ranch outside of Sundown Valley. Sundown Ranch. The owner is a single man with triplets."

"Nannying? Where did that come from? This is the first I've heard of such a thing."

"I know, I know, but hear me out." Now she was sounding like Wade Trudeau.

She told her dad of finding the card on a community bulletin board and the basics of her interview with Wade Trudeau.

"Two men and three babies," her dad mused. "The set up sounds like an old Tom Selleck movie."

She chuckled. "At first, I was going to refuse, but then Mr. Trudeau asked me to consider taking the job just for the summer."

"Is this something that interests you? Living on a ranch in the country nearly three hours from all your friends and family, confined with three little ones 24/7?"

Now that he put it that way, she worried. Could she do it? Did she want to? Would her back hold up from toting around three toddlers?

"Not 24/7, Dad. I can choose my days off."

"That's something, at least."

While they talked, a cardinal landed on the guardrail

a few feet away. She'd heard that a redbird was a love letter from God, a reminder of a deceased loved one, meant to bring comfort.

She didn't know if she believed in such things or not, but the thought was lovely, uplifting.

Watching birds, especially cardinals, from her hospital window had been a pastime when her body was too broken to do much else. The red birds never failed to cheer her, bringing thoughts of her mother. And of Tristan.

"I don't know if *interests* is the right word, Dad, but I have to work again. I *need* to work, if only to prove I can. A nanny job in the rural beauty and peace of the Kiamichi could be a way to ease in gradually and regain more of my strength. It might help reset my addled brain, too."

"I'm not trying to discourage you, honey. You have a gift with children."

She knew that much was true. Children were her calling. The tragedy had stolen too much from her already. She couldn't allow it to take any more.

"You said yourself I need a change of pace, a change of scenery. That's why we agreed for me to come to the mountains."

"You've always loved the Kiamichi. When your mom was alive and we'd spend vacations there, you were never happier."

"That's true. I love this area. Looking at the mountains, which I'm doing right now, and hiking in the quiet woods, makes me feel closer to God."

"And makes you poetic. Remember all the pretty poems you wrote when we were camping?"

"That was a long time ago." She hadn't felt like writing anything except lesson plans in years. Now, even those were in the past.

"Maybe you need to get back to that place. Writing can be cathartic."

"Are you telling me to take the job?"

"You know me better than that, Kyra. You're a grown woman. A brilliant, well-educated woman with a good head on your shoulders. You've been making your own decisions for years."

"Always with your wise counsel," she said.

"Except for Sean Allred."

"Dad, please. Don't mention *that* mistake. After the accident, he disappeared faster than evaporating mist."

She still ached at her boyfriend's reaction.

"The tragedy scared him."

"Yes, the coward." She and Sean had been edging toward forever, but after the tornado, he'd stopped calling, stopped coming to see her. "He was scared I'd be confined to a wheelchair, and he didn't want to deal with a disabled girlfriend. *Couldn't* deal with it, I guess."

While she was fighting to walk again, Sean had started dating someone else.

So much for true love.

"I hope you've forgiven him."

"Forgiven, yes, but any love that might have been developing between us left when he did."

"He hurt you. I understand that. I was pretty upset with him myself."

"Dad. Let it go. I have."

Romance was so far off her radar as to be nonexistent. For the last year, she'd been regaining her health. Maybe in the future she'd be interested in finding her special someone, but not now. Not anytime soon.

In this season of her life, her total focus and goal was to get mentally and physically strong enough to teach again.

Her dad cleared his throat. "Back to our topic. Those little ones would be blessed to have you, but living in the same house with two strange men? I'm not comfortable with that. What do you know about them?"

She told him about the bunkhouse.

"Perhaps a change of occupations is what I need, Dad, at least for a while until the episodes go away for good."

Cold sweats, shaking and, the very worst, flashbacks to those horrific hours buried beneath a mountain of rubble.

"Have you had another one?"

"Not the flashbacks, no." The others she could handle. "Thank the merciful Lord, and you. I know you're praying for me."

"Daily. My entire congregation, as well. Healing of the mind often takes longer than healing the body." He'd shifted to his counseling roll, something he'd done frequently over the last year. "Give yourself that time, Kyra."

"So you agree this might be God's answer for now?"

"The bigger question is, do you think it is?"

"Maybe. I called Wade Trudeau's references, including his pastor. They all said the same thing. He's had a hard time the last couple of years, but he's a Christian man as solid as the mountain."

He hadn't looked or acted too solid this morning. But she didn't tell her father that.

"Who's his pastor? I know a few down that way. Maybe we've met at a conference or retreat. We preachers run in a pretty small circle. I could give him a call, pastor-to-pastor."

Even though she'd already spoken to the man, her father knew the right questions to ask. And as he said, pastor-to-pastor was a special bond.

Kyra opened the note she'd folded in half. "I have it right here, Dad. Grab a pencil."

She heard her dad rummaging at his desk. This time of day, he worked in his office, taking care of a hundred duties no one knew lead pastors did.

"Go ahead when ready," he said.

She rattled off the name and phone number.

"Pastor Blake Cloud," he said. "The name sounds familiar. Let me give him a call and get back to you."

"Thanks, Daddy. I love you."

"You, too, honey."

They hung up, and Kyra climbed into the car, marveling that she'd gone from practically running away from Sundown Ranch to leaning toward living there for the next three months.

The attraction had to be the triplets. It certainly wasn't the man. Other than being pathetic, he had no charisma whatsoever.

Thank goodness.

Wade Trudeau was *so* not her type. She preferred smooth businessmen in suits, not wild, unshaven cowboys in dusty boots.

But those sweet little babies. She couldn't forget them.

Maybe Wade was doing his best, but he was trying to juggle childcare with ranching and the two didn't mix. Three active toddlers were a full-time job for any one person. Preferably two people.

She wondered how long Wade had cared for the triplets alone. Had his wife recently left? Or had he been their sole caregiver since birth?

Okay, now she was feeling sorry for the man. But more than that, she felt sorry for the triplets. They needed time and attention Wade could not give them. Not if he wanted to make a living on his ranch.

They needed a mother.

Within five minutes, her cell phone jangled.

Her dad was calling.

And Kyra's decision was made.

Chapter Three

"I blew it, Bowie."

Wade ripped off a giant, annoyed bite as if to punish the ham sandwich. While he chewed, he scooped Caden's sippy cup off the floor for the umpteenth time and thumped it onto the highchair.

Three sets of messy hands alternately shoved food into their mouths and slapped their high-chair trays containing said food. The floor, as usual, was a mess.

Maybe he should get a house dog. He could let Pudge inside to play clean-up duty. The blue heeler would love that, and a judicious swipe of the cow dog's tongue would save Wade or Bowie another sweep-and-mop job.

A win-win.

Not too sanitary but efficient.

"What happened?" Bowie put down his sandwich and reached for his tea glass.

"A woman showed up out of the blue to inquire about the nanny job."

"Sounds good so far."

"Except she'd gotten one of my cards from somewhere, and the ad asked for a housekeeper. Which we need. That wasn't a lie." He stared at the lettuce poking out of his sandwich and grimaced. "But I didn't exactly mention the nanny thing in the ad. Or the triplets."

He glanced up to see Bowie's reaction.

He didn't get much of one. That was Bowie's way.

Though plenty of women thought the Cajun cousin was a tall, dark and handsome dreamboat, Bowie seldom gave anyone a second look. He liked women. He was just quiet and reserved with a cautious streak a mile wide and ten miles long.

Wade knew the reasons for that caution, though, like Sabrina, the past wounds were seldom discussed. As in never.

His cousin took a long drink of sweet tea before asking, "Why not?"

"For obvious reasons, Sherlock." Bowie could be a little dense when it came to social cues, another reason he didn't date much. "The mention of three kids seems to terrify people."

"So she went running."

"Not at first. For a minute, I thought I had her on the hook."

Bowie crunched a chip, waiting for the punch line.

"She asked about their mother." He shot a look at his motherless babies. Women. They stole your heart and then crushed it. At least one woman. The woman he'd adored and treated like a queen.

Worst of all was what she'd done to their triplets.

Hurting him was one thing. He was a man, an adult. But how could he forgive what she'd done to his babies?

Another reason Bowie was women-shy. He'd lived through Wade's disaster.

"Uh-oh. Wrong turn."

"Yeah. I might have overreacted. Even though Kyra took my references, I'll never hear from her again."

Abby turned her cup upside down. Milk drip-dripped onto the high-chair tray.

Bowie calmly reached out and took the cup.

Abby howled.

Wade handed her a piece of cheese.

"So back to square one, Bowie. Looks like the ranch will be on you and Riley for a while longer." Wade didn't know how the dependable ranch hand and Bowie had managed by themselves since the triplets' birth. He, though part owner, had been pretty much useless on the ranch, and that had to change now that spring was here and the workload increased exponentially. "I'm gonna text Yates again, ask him one more time to come home and take his rightful place."

It wouldn't be the first time he'd tried to contact his wayward brother. More like the hundredth.

He whipped out his cell phone and scrolled to the number Yates had reluctantly given him three years ago.

"Think he'll answer?"

"Doubt it, but I have to try. Sundown Ranch is his, too. We need his help, especially now."

Yates had joined the military shortly after the accident that had cost their youngest brother his life. Yates blamed Wade for Trent's death, and he was right. Wade carried a load of guilt, along with the grief. But he'd already lost one brother. Losing Yates, too, was unthinkable.

He wouldn't give up until his maverick brother came home.

His thumbs raced across the digital keyboard, asking his brother to return and take his place on the ranch that was one-third his. Saying a prayer, Wade hit Send and then pocketed the device.

Bowie scraped his chair away from the table to retrieve a fallen or tossed sippy cup. Tossing the cup was a game all three babies found wildly entertaining.

"Teenagers look for work in summer," his cousin said as he plunked the sippy on Caden's tray. "Hire one of them to babysit."

Wade scowled. "I don't want a kid looking after the triplets!"

Bowie lifted an eyebrow, silent, then got up to fix himself another sandwich.

"All right." Wade waved his half-eaten sandwich. "I see your point. Beggars can't be choosers. But I'll hire a teenager only as a last resort. Someone we know from church. I'm holding out a while longer for an adult with experience. Like Kyra Mason."

"You keep talking about her." Bowie tilted away from the open refrigerator to look at him with those knowing black eyes. "Was she pretty?"

Wade's scowl grew deeper. The redhead's picture rose in his brain, all prim, proper and pretty. Fact of the business, he'd thought of her all morning. Of the sweet way she'd played with Abby. Of how good she smelled. Of her fresh, wholesome appearance and that glossy red hair.

He, who'd sworn off women for the rest of his life, couldn't get one small female out of his head.

Because she was the perfect candidate for the job. Not because he found her attractive.

"Doesn't matter. She's long gone. Probably hightailed it back to Tulsa as fast as that itty-bitty car could take her."

"Tulsa?" Bowie slid a knife full of mayo across a slice of wheat bread. "Not a local?"

"I know what you're thinking. City girl. What was she doing down here in the bojacks, anyway?"

A city girl would never stick around. Just ask him. He knew from painful experience. You could take the girl out of the city, but you couldn't take the city out of the girl. The old saying was a cliché for a very good reason.

He grabbed for the wet wipes in the center of the table and ripped off a few for the yellow macaroni and cheese Benjamin had smeared on his baby-bird chest.

In return, Ben offered Wade a bite from his messy little fingers. Wade pretended to eat, making gobble-up noises like the Cookie Monster. All three babies chortled.

Man, they were awesome, his three cute nuggets, even if they kept him hopping day and night.

His cell phone chirped.

Wade fished the phone from his back pocket.

"Sundown Ranch. Wade speaking."

His pulse leaped. Then his hopes rose. He listened and then spoke for a moment before hanging up.

If his adrenaline jacked any higher, he'd be a helium balloon.

"Well?" Bowie asked, pointing the mayo knife. "Your face is red. Who was it?"

"Kyra Mason."

Bowie tilted his head as he screwed the lid onto the mayo jar. "The redhead who ran away?"

"Yes. She's on her way to look at the bunkhouse."

"For what? To live in?" Bowie stuck the condiment jar in the fridge.

"Yeah. I sort of made her an offer. A place to live away from the main house and us guys."

"You want her to live in the old rundown bunkhouse that nobody's used in forever? A city girl?" He whistled softly. "That's not good, cuz."

Wade slammed a hand through his hair, then realized he had macaroni and cheese on his fingers.

"Grab the cleaning supplies. I'll get the triplets. We've got work to do. Fast."

Kyra arrived at the Sundown Ranch to discover two cowboys motioning to her from the porch of a weathered, rustic building.

Was *that* the bunkhouse?

Rather than turn left from the long graveled driveway toward the ranch's main house, she turned right down a very short overgrown path and parked next to the sad-looking wooden structure.

For one very long moment, she questioned her decision to come back.

The hopeful expression on Wade Trudeau's face got her out of the car.

God had a plan, and that plan included a summer on the Sundown Ranch. After her phone call to accept the summer-only job, she'd driven home to Tulsa for some of her belongings.

"Did you have a safe trip?" Wade's tone was falsely jovial.

He must have seen her hesitation.

Kyra stepped up on the porch. A board was missing at one end, but otherwise the floor felt solid.

One positive thing.

Her gaze roamed over the tired building. Hopefully, the interior was better.

"Yes. Thank you. My car is loaded down."

One brown eyebrow jacked up. "Wouldn't take much."

Was he making fun of her cute car?

The three of them stood awkwardly while the building creaked and the wind ruffled the weeds growing around the steps. One lonely stray daffodil waved from the tangled mess.

The splash of yellow was exactly the impetus she needed.

"You must be Bowie," Kyra finally said, offering a hand to a tall, handsome man in a gray cowboy hat and dusty boots.

"Yes, ma'am." He wiped one hand down his jeans' leg before shaking hers.

He was obviously the cousin. The familial similarities to Wade were undeniable, though Bowie's coloring was darker. They were both tall and fit and bore the same sculpted jaw and strong cheekbones.

Handsome.

"I didn't think you'd come back," Wade said.

She smiled. "I guess I'm a surprise, then."

He let out a gusty breath. "A good one."

One of the triplets, she wasn't sure which one, toddled out the open door, dragging a baby blanket behind.

"Is this the bunkhouse?"

"Yes." Both men seemed to be guarding the doorway. "We're letting it air while we clean up some."

"May I see the inside?"

"Oh, sure. Yes. Sure." Wade's stuttering reply didn't reassure her.

He hoisted the advancing baby under the armpits and swung him or her through the doorway.

Kyra stepped inside behind the man and child. The other two babies, the identical boys, she saw now, played with a pile of toys in one corner of the long, narrow room.

Abby toddled to her brothers, chattering something only the three of them understood. Ben—or was it Caden?—offered the little girl a play cell phone. She held it to her ear and babbled.

Kyra let her gaze drift from the babies to the bunkhouse interior.

The place smelled musty. And dusty. So much so she coughed.

In one corner, directly inside the long rectangular room, sat a scarred wooden table and chairs for two. The other side was empty with swirls of dust on the flooring as if someone had recently moved out the furniture. A chair or couch, perhaps?

A few more steps into the space and two rows of heavy oak bunks bracketed the sides of the room.

Dust covered everything. Dirt daubers' red mud nests plastered the walls.

Were there mice? She shuddered. She hated mice.

Something in her expression must have warned him because Wade said, "As I mentioned this morning, we haven't used the bunkhouse in a long time."

He wiped a finger across the end of a bunk. Dust motes swirled. "The place is a little dusty."

A little? Cobwebs hung from windows so dirty as to be opaque. The old curtains needed to be burned. Their color was indistinguishable.

An attempt had been made recently to sweep and mop the long wooden floor, a useless gesture given that the walls and ceilings needed to be cleaned and dirt daubers removed.

The mattresses on the double row of bunk beds, thankfully, were encased in plastic.

Could she live in this?

"We'll clean it up. Don't you worry." Wade sounded desperate.

Once again, Kyra felt sorry for him. Her tender heart was getting the best of her.

"I don't do mice," Kyra blurted.

"No signs of them. Nothing in here to attract them. Right, Bowie?"

Bowie nodded.

That was something, anyway.

"The bathroom and kitchenette are functional." Wade pointed toward the opposite end of the rectangular room where an alcove divided the space.

Kyra moved to the alcove, her footsteps thudding against the wood floor.

Wade followed. She could feel his anxiety.

Turning to the right of the alcove, she glanced inside a small bathroom, which didn't appear too disgusting. The window had been opened and fresh air flowed inside.

A full bottle of Lysol cleaner perched on the vanity next to a stack of cleaning rags.

The double vanity surprised her, but if several ranch hands had lived in the bunkhouse, two sinks probably hadn't been enough.

"Think this will work?" Wade asked, eager, hopeful, though the worry frown between his eyes expressed his real feelings. He was afraid she'd bolt.

So was she.

"Let's see the kitchenette."

She rounded the doorway to the left of the alcove.

A tiny kitchenette consisted of a greasy two-burner stove, no oven and a dorm-sized refrigerator bearing dirty handprints. She wondered how long they'd been there.

Above the appliances, a row of dusty shelves sat empty.

Toward the center of the space, beneath a window that overlooked a vast green field with mountains in the distance, was a small bar-sized sink. A rust stain ringed the drain. Underneath was a storage cabinet with a single drawer. Small but functional.

"You'll take most of your meals at the main house with us. If you want to," he hurried to add. "I could use your help feeding the triplets."

"Of course." Once cleaned, the kitchenette would serve adequately for snacks and morning coffee. "Is there a coffeepot? Or a microwave?"

"I'll get new ones. We tossed the others." He grimaced. "They were in pretty bad shape."

She could only imagine anything in worse shape than the stove.

"Bowie's good at mechanical things," he went on as if pointing out the positives would convince her to stay. "He's checked out the appliances and bathroom fixtures. The AC is good. Fridge is working. Everything's a go."

No, everything was not a go. Making this building livable would take hours, maybe days.

"I—" Kyra considered turning down the offer, or at least postponing her start date until the bunkhouse was in better condition.

Without saying as much, she walked back into the bunk area.

If she lived here, she'd move the table to this end near the kitchenette. The light from the window on the east would be pleasant in the mornings.

And maybe she'd add an easy chair and a TV on the other side, a mini-living room of sorts.

A big area rug in the center of the room would brighten things up and make the room cozy. New curtains, too.

One of the triplets waddled over and offered her a touch-and-feel baby book. Kyra crouched low, took the book and the baby's finger, rubbing it across a wooly sheep.

"Sheep are soft."

So was her heart.

This baby needed her.

She read a few more pages, guiding the child to touch each one, then rose to her feet and faced Wade.

"Let's focus on this area and the bath for today. The kitchen and windows can wait. I'll help."

"You're staying?" Wade's blue eyes widened.

Bowie chuckled but didn't say anything. She'd noticed he didn't talk much.

"Once the place is clean, you promise to fix it up? New curtains, rugs and anything else I deem necessary to make it livable."

"Anything you want. Anything."

"You might regret those words." She wasn't fancy or a germophobe. A special-needs teacher couldn't afford to be, but she wanted clean, organized and functional. "I'll take every weekend off and July Fourth."

"Agreed. Bowie and I can hold the fort."

"And I want new locks on the door and the only key to the bunkhouse."

If the demand offended him, he didn't react.

"Agreed, but you have my word that no one on this ranch will bother you. They try, and they answer to me."

"Thank you. I appreciate that." She also kept a baseball bat beside her bed, and she was not afraid to use it. In college, she'd been a pretty solid intramural softball hitter.

"So, it's a deal?" Wade asked. "You'll take the job? Move in here tonight?"

One of the babies, Benjamin, she thought, reached his arms toward her. How could she resist? She lifted his chubby body against her shoulder. He patted her hair.

He was such a precious lamb, even though his diaper sagged and his face was dirty.

"For the summer." She smoothed a hand over Benjamin's soft cap of hair, spotting what appeared to be a glob of yellow cheese.

"Three months." Three months she hoped she didn't regret. "Until school starts again."

She hoped and prayed that by late August she'd be ready to walk into a classroom full of children.

Wade looked at his hand, wiped it on his shirt and

held it out to her. Kyra put her fingers in his to shake on the deal.

His palm was calloused and rough and swallowed hers. She liked the feeling. And if tiny tingles played over her nerve endings, she blamed them on the back injury. She'd had plenty of tingles after the tragedy as feeling had slowly returned to her battered body.

The electric charges certainly couldn't be attraction.

She withdrew her hand. The tingles remained. "Let's get busy getting this bunkhouse clean. Otherwise, you're renting me a hotel room tonight."

Wade blinked several times.

Bowie laughed.

She gave them her sweetest smile, grabbed a bucket and headed for the bathroom.

Chapter Four

Wade pulled his pickup truck to a stop beside the bunkhouse and hopped out. He had a boatload of ranch work to do but his number one priority today, other than the triplets, was keeping the new nanny happy and in residence.

She'd stayed in the bunkhouse last night, though he had seen in her expression that she was less than impressed with his idea of appropriate nanny living quarters.

City girls had no comprehension of roughing it.

But he wouldn't complain. She'd taken the job. She was here. Best of all, she was doing okay with the triplets. So far. But it was early yet. Three toddlers was a lot for anyone. A woman without kids, even a teacher, couldn't know the challenges that lay ahead.

Which meant Wade had to make the bunkhouse as comfortable as possible, a refuge for Kyra to escape to each evening when he took charge of the babies. They mostly slept through the night now, anyway. He could handle the times they didn't. She, however, had to rise before six o'clock to take over while he headed out to work.

Only Caden had cried this morning when Wade left the house. Kyra had swooped in with a silly face, a tickle and a sippy cup, and the little guy had hushed up before Wade got to the back door.

He hoped her enthusiasm and energy didn't wane. It certainly had with the last two nannies. Fast.

He could not let that happen.

Wade pulled the handle of the tailgate and it fell open with a metal slam. The sound echoed in the spring sunshine, flushing a flock of blackbirds.

Pudge, his cow dog and loyal companion, leaped from the back of the truck to the ground, tongue lolling happily, looking at Wade as if to say, *What now, boss? Can I chase something? Got a cow that needs herding? Let me at 'em. Let me at 'em.*

That dog loved to herd cows and ride in the truck. "Soon, pal. We're vaccinating later today. You'll get to have your fun."

Three barns were within eyeshot beyond the house. Wade glanced toward them in search of help before recalling that his ranch hands were otherwise occupied.

Both Bowie and Riley were moving hay to the ranch's west forty acres and checking on the pregnant mamas. Wade didn't expect to see either one of them until evening.

Ah, well, no big deal. He'd get these bunkhouse items delivered and head for the barn to unload the rest. It wouldn't be the first time he'd worked alone. It was, however, the first time since Miss Janey left that he'd been able to work outside for any length of time.

Leaving the triplets for even a short period was not an option. Anything could happen. Bowie helped out in short spurts, but the babies were Wade's responsibility. He refused to impose on his easygoing cousin any more than necessary. Bowie loved the babies but he, an unconfirmed bachelor, knew less about kids than Wade did and wasn't eager to learn.

Hiring a nanny took a heavy weight off his shoulders, and it felt good to be back in the saddle, so to speak. Which he literally would be later today.

First, to make the nanny happy. Or at least happier.

Please, Lord, make her happy. I haven't been too successful in the make-a-woman-happy department.

Not that he was interested in making Kyra happy as in girlfriend happy. He only wanted her to be content and to fall so in love with his triplets that she couldn't leave them until they were a little older. Say maybe eighteen or twenty.

He snorted at the ridiculous thought.

The impossible dream.

Dragging the boxes toward the end of the truck bed, he hoisted the heaviest and started toward the bunkhouse.

The door stood open. He wasn't invading anyone's privacy.

He hoped.

He stepped inside and hollered, "Kyra? You in here?"

No reply, so he figured she and the littles were still in the main house. He'd left them in the kitchen this morning, having a breakfast he'd cooked before Kyra arrived.

She'd had to knock on the back door.

He needed to give her a house key.

With a groan, he recalled the new lock and key he'd promised for the bunkhouse.

Another trip to town. Maybe tomorrow. Not today. Too much catch-up work to do.

Toting the microwave to the kitchenette, Wade paused. The space still looked pathetic, particularly the cook stove. Better not set up anything until the place was clean.

With a sigh, he set the box on the scarred table in the main room, grabbed some rags and cleaner and got to work.

After running hot water in the tiny sink, he dumped in enough Lysol to make himself cough. The cleaner smelled great. It was just strong.

Using his considerable upper body strength, he started scrubbing grates while eliminating enough grease to lubricate his cab tractor.

Man, ranch hands were slobs.

A woman expected nice things. *Clean* things.

"I can do this, Wade."

At the soft female voice, Wade swung around. His belly did something weird. Sort of a jitterbug.

He ignored it. Mostly.

Kyra stood in the doorway. A baby on each hip, she held the other one by the hand. How did she manage that? It had taken him weeks to figure out the best way to herd/carry all three at once. He'd even considered training Pudge to help with the herding.

"I got your microwave." He nudged his chin in that direction.

"Thank you." She slid the babies to the floor, which he noticed looked a lot cleaner than it had last night. He and Bowie had swiped at the dust with a mop before she'd arrived, but now the floor looked shiny in the sunlight shooting in from the east window.

"Did you stay up half the night cleaning?"

Her grin was sheepish. "Maybe."

"Well, don't. I'll knock off early each evening until we get the place in shape. You shouldn't have to do this all yourself and watch the triplets, too."

"We cleared out the worst of the dirt and yuck last night, so I feel comfortable bringing the babies out here while I clean and organize." She ran a hand over the top of the microwave box. "If you're okay with me working out here with them present."

"Sure. Fine. Whatever you want to do." Yesterday, he'd worried about exposing the triplets to the dust, too, but a man did what a man had to do.

They'd been so dirty last night when he'd helped Kyra bathe them that they'd had to change the water between kids.

He was kind of embarrassed about that. He hoped she didn't think he was a negligent dad.

"I'm here," he said. "Might as well fumigate this stove."

She laughed and reached for a pair of rubber gloves he'd actually remembered to bring to the cabin last night. "It is bad, isn't it?"

"I should have bought a new one while I was in Sundown Valley." He'd been right there in the home store. He could have bought a stove, the lock, whatever. "You'll need to make a list for my next trip."

He hoped she didn't break the bank. So far, she'd not been demanding, but this was only day one. And she *was* a female.

Kyra cast a watchful glance at the triplets now toddling around the long mostly empty bunkhouse. His trio had a habit of getting into anything they shouldn't. Watching was duty numero uno.

A clothes basket of toys he'd never seen before was pushed against one wall. Abby headed toward them, babbling.

"No need for a new stove," she said. "This will do. It's only for three months."

His hopeful mood plummeted.

Oh. Yeah. Rats. Three lousy months.

In the confined space, she managed to take the two burners from him and dump them in the sink of water. "Let them soak. I'll use oven cleaner on them tonight."

He screwed up his face. "Do I have oven cleaner?"

She laughed. Which had been his intention. He sure

liked the sound. Warm and light. And when she laughed, her eyes sparkled. He liked that, too.

"I don't know," she said. "Do you?"

"Probably not. Unless Janey, our previous house-keeper, left some in the kitchen."

"Don't worry about it. I'll look. I haven't had a chance to do much cleaning in the main house yet."

He stared at her, which wasn't a hardship. Her red hair was pulled back in a bouncy ponytail, which better displayed her apple cheekbones and slightly tilted nose.

Not that he was noticing. But he sure liked the color of her hair.

"You have your hands full here. For now, Bowie and I can shovel the house out if needed."

"What about dinner? Isn't cooking part of my job description, too?"

"We got it for now. Give yourself a few days to get settled with the bunkhouse and the triplets."

"I prefer to pull my weight, but that's thoughtful of you."

Thoughtful? No. Pure self-preservation.

He'd do about anything to keep her from jumping in that tiny blue car and running away to Tulsa.

They worked in silence for a few minutes. He wanted to say something but couldn't think of anything intelligent. The quiet was a little awkward.

Finally, he blurted, "I bought coffee."

Her back was turned to him as she scrubbed the shelves under the sink. She pivoted on a pair of tan canvas shoes that would be filthy by nightfall.

"What about a coffeepot?"

"That's what I meant. Coffeepot." His brain wasn't working properly. Likely because he'd actually slept most of last night. He wasn't accustomed to solid sleep.

"One of those pod coffee makers," he said, "and the coffee to go with it." He might have tossed in some tea and a few other pod drinks in case she preferred those.

She smiled up at him. "Perfect."

"It's in the truck. I'll get it." He started out the door, stopping to kiss each nugget on the head. Benjamin ended up following him onto the porch.

He grabbed the other boxes and, using his knee as an extra hand, guided his son back into the cabin.

Kyra met him halfway to the door. "I thought I'd lost him. They move fast."

"Truer words were never spoken." He hoped she understood how important every second was when it came to watching three little ones.

Though her references glowed, she'd worked with school-age kids, not babies. Besides, he didn't know her well enough yet to fully trust her with his most prized possessions.

He felt a little guilty about that, but he'd feel worse if something happened to one of the triplets.

After sliding the remaining boxes onto the only table in the place, he raked a hand through his hair, and said, "I'm sorry to abandon you."

"Go. You have work."

But he didn't want to go. He wanted to stay right here with her and those three babies.

It was probably that trust thing.

But something about Kyra...

Get a grip, Trudeau. City girl. Three months and she's gone. Don't be dumb. You've been dumb before. Don't be dumb again.

She might be pretty and personable. She might be kind to him and his children. That was what he wanted. That was the deal.

The *only* deal.

With a one-fingered salute, he backed away and loped to the truck. Pudge hopped into the bed and hung his happy canine head over the side while Wade slammed the tailgate and jumped into the truck.

Get back to work. And don't even think about the pretty nanny.

Kyra was nothing if not a good employee. That was the way her dad had raised her, and that was the way she'd always worked. A day's work for a day's pay, he'd said, and she agreed. Up until the back injury had sidelined her, she'd been the teacher who'd gone the extra mile, working before and after school and sometimes weekends.

Now, she was praying to make it through the first day.

Her back ached, and she longed to lie down and take a nap.

To make matters worse, she'd been awake half the night listening to the strange noises. That was why she'd been up cleaning. Not because she was a clean freak, even though she was, but because of the noises.

The coyote howls had been the worst. She didn't hear those in a Tulsa suburb. On camping trips, yes, but those days had been years ago when she was a kid with her family right beside her in the tent. She'd never even noticed the night sounds back then.

She wasn't afraid, but the howling had disturbed her sleep. Not to mention the strange bed in a strange building that barely passed as livable. And the odd mixture of cleaning products and dust annoying her nose. She had a powerful sense of smell.

Gritting her teeth against the ache in her back, Kyra hoisted two babies, took the other by the hand, and left the bunkhouse. She'd cleaned and rearranged all her body could take for now.

Nap time couldn't come fast enough. Not only for the babies. For herself.

Maybe she was trying to do too much too soon. Maybe her body wasn't ready for this much work. Or for dealing with small children.

Three toddlers were a lot for someone healing from a broken back. Then there was the unbearable thought that she might accidentally let down her guard and allow something to happen to one of them.

A memory flashed in her head. Screaming, whimpering voices, followed by the awful silence.

She'd been responsible that day, and she'd failed.

With a hard shudder, Kyra blocked the horror from her mind before the memory became reality, before the flashbacks hit her and she lost all sense of time and place.

Nothing would happen to the triplets. She must be vigilant, even if that required sitting beside their cribs while they slept and watching every step they took.

"Help me do this, Lord." She whispered a prayer she'd prayed numerous times in the last twenty-four hours. "Protect these children. Guard my heart and mind. Strengthen my body."

She'd come to Sundown Ranch to get her life back, to prove she could work again, that she could live a normal life. Most of all to prove that being with children wouldn't trigger the PTSD.

What if, while she was alone with the triplets, she suffered a flashback and lost touch with reality?

If Wade knew about the disaster that had brought her here, would he have hired her? Would he trust her with his babies?

She hadn't had an episode in months. But what if she did?

She shook her head to dispel the nagging worries.

Be careful for nothing; but in every thing by prayer and supplication with thanksgiving let your requests be made known unto God. And the peace of God, which passeth all understanding, shall keep your hearts and your minds in Christ Jesus.

As a kid, she'd grown weary of memorizing scripture. Now she was grateful when the exact words she needed flooded in.

The peace of God *would* guard her heart and mind.

"Thank you, Mom." For it had been her mother who had assigned a memory verse per week. "Thank you, Lord, for the reminders."

Now, if she could only follow the very good scriptural advice. She'd prayed. Now to stop worrying and accept God's peace.

Benjamin the bold yanked from her grip to chase a butterfly. She let the other two wiggle worms slide to the ground, and they followed Ben, their chubby legs and arms pumping. Occasionally, one fell down, only to pop up and head out again.

Adorable.

A lot of work, but so, so cute.

She pulled her cell phone from her back jeans' pocket and snapped some photos to show Wade later.

A text box popped up. Amy, her best friend, checking on her, offering to commandeer some guys and a pickup truck if she wanted to bring any of her furniture from Tulsa.

Amy could always commandeer any number of guys. Kyra wondered what she'd think of two real cowboys?

Smiling, she dashed off a reply, then took a few more photos.

When the trio tired of the futile chase, Kyra herded them toward the back door of the main house. Herding distractible toddlers wasn't easy, but it gave her back a break.

How had Wade done this alone, for the most part, while still running a ranch and handling all the other chores a home and children required? Yes, his cousin lived here, but as he'd told her, the triplets were his children and his responsibility. He carried the load.

Her sympathy for him grew.

He wasn't a negligent dad. He had too much on his plate.

She planned to take some of those duties off his wide muscled shoulders.

That was what he was paying her for.

Never mind that she'd felt some tingly moments of attraction for the rancher. Watching a man gently diaper a baby shouldn't be such a turn-on.

She laughed at the ridiculous thought. All three toddlers looked up and grinned. Four teeth, two on top and two on bottom, showed in all three mouths.

Her heart squeezed.

Once inside the house, she settled the ABC trio on a questionably clean kitchen floor with a yogurt snack pouch.

With the babies momentarily occupied, she explored the kitchen cabinets, discovered a slow cooker and searched the freezer for something easy to prepare for dinner.

One less thing for Wade to handle.

She mentally patted herself on the back for the idea.

Even if Wade had promised to help, a meal that cooked itself would make life easier on all of them.

Though not an accomplished chef, she had a cell phone and could read a recipe.

After scrolling the internet, Kyra put together what she hoped would be a rancher-filling meal and plugged in the Crock-Pot. Would it be enough? She'd never cooked for three adults and three toddlers before.

By then, Abby was crying and rubbing her eyes. Caden needed a fresh diaper. And Ben pounded his empty pouch against the refrigerator, apparently demanding more food. At the top of his lungs.

Wade hadn't given her a schedule. Did he think an unexpected, unprepared nanny automatically knew what to feed toddlers? Or when to put them down for a nap?

She didn't, but she'd figure it out. Flexibility was the name of the game in the teaching profession.

She glanced at the food-prep mess on the counters, then at the needy toddlers. And there was this sticky floor to consider.

The back doorknob rattled. Kyra froze. The toddlers, on the other hand, amped up a few hundred decibels.

Their dad appeared in the doorway.

Kyra's stomach dipped, a car-over-a-high-hill dip. Not attraction. Definitely not. She'd been startled by his unexpected return to the house. That was all.

"How's it going?" he said over the cacophony.

Caden, the stinky one, rushed toward Wade, lost his balance and splatted against the tile. His howl rivaled last night's coyotes.

Wade went to his haunches to lift the boy into a hug. Abby took this as a good sign and joined them, consoling her crying brother with a pat or two on the face. Ben continued to yell from the fridge.

Over the din, Kyra wanted to answer Wade's question with one word. *Chaos.* She didn't. If Wade was already back in the house after his visit to the bunkhouse cabin, he was checking on her, making sure she could properly care for his children.

At the moment, she had her doubts.

"We're figuring things out," she said. "I could use a schedule."

He looked up. Her stomach did that dipping thing again.

He really was a good-looking man.

"For the babies?" he asked over Abby's skinny top-of-the-head ponytail. "Don't have one. If they're hungry, I feed them. If they're sleepy or cranky, I put them in their cribs."

"Oh." She was a schedule kind of person. A list-maker. A notetaker. Organization was the key to sanity. "I really need a schedule."

Wade rose from the floor, Caden in his arms. He patted the fussing child's back, his wide rancher's hand against the small cotton-clad body. Incongruous and sweet.

The baby sniffled and rubbed his wet face against the cowboy's blue shirt. Blue, a color that made Wade's eyes even more noticeable. Today, the pretty irises were less bloodshot, and the cowboy had shaved.

Not that she intended to notice.

But she did, and that bothered her a little.

Employee. Employer. Nothing else.

She wanted to keep this job all summer, not get fired. Wade had been more than clear about his attitude toward romance.

"We can make a schedule. Sure," he was saying, and Kyra mentally slapped her focus from the man's good looks to the toddlers. "Or you can make one to please yourself. Whatever works best for you."

What would work best for her was to stop noticing him so much. Here was a man with an ex-wife he obviously still loved or he wouldn't freak out when she was mentioned. And Kyra was a woman trying to get her life back on track. She couldn't chance adding another heartache to the mix.

"When do they usually nap?"

"Anytime after they eat lunch."

"They don't take bottles anymore? Right?"

He made a face. "No, thank the merciful Lord. Janey weaned them before she left. I'm not sure I could have managed that little trick on my own. All that crying and whining." He gave a fake shudder. And there Kyra went again, noticing those wide shoulders. "Brutal. Especially Ben. He's a demanding little critter."

Kyra smiled. "I noticed. Ben the bold. Abby the amiable talker and Caden the cuddler, maybe a little timid and tender."

"You nailed them." He looked pleased, which made her pleased, too.

Caden had now stopped crying. Kyra reached to take him from Wade. "He needs to be changed."

"Probably the others do, too." He hoisted the remaining two. "Let's do this."

"This is my job, Wade. You have the ranch."

He shrugged. "My babies."

He followed her to the nursery, and in no time, he'd changed his two while she was still wrestling to keep a naked but clean Caden in one place.

Suddenly, a hand appeared above Caden's face, rattling a set of plastic keys. The baby stilled, eyes watchful, and then latched onto them.

"You're a genius." Kyra quickly slid the diaper under Caden and secured the tabs.

"Practice. Lots and lots."

"How long have you done this by yourself?"

"This time? About three months. Since their first birthday. Janey, our nanny, left the next week. Her brother got sick."

Kyra wanted to ask how long the triplets' mother had been gone.

Lest she hit a nerve again, she chose her wording carefully. "Have you been on your own with them since birth?"

His face closed up. "Mostly." A new tension ebbed from him. He backed away from the changing table. "Gotta get to work."

"Wait. Wade." She lifted Caden into her arms, still zipping his onesie with the opposite hand. "I didn't mean to upset you."

He offered a tight, and most certainly fake, smile. "Not upset. Busy." He saluted in that charming way of his. One finger. "Later."

Abby ran after him, yelling something that sounded like, "Da-da-da-da-da."

Ben screamed and threw a stuffed monkey.

Caden snuggled into her shoulder and sucked his index finger.

Yes, indeed. For a long time, she'd refused to discuss Sean. So she knew the signs. Wade Trudeau still nursed a broken heart.

Chapter Five

Wade scooped another spoonful of the casserole Kyra had prepared for dinner. He'd not expected her to cook for them—not so soon, anyway. But, man, when he'd walked in the back door exhausted and smelled that food cooking, his mouth had watered and his belly had done a happy dance.

She'd set the dining room table, too. He couldn't remember the last time they'd used that room. Back when Sabrina had been in residence, he figured, though he didn't like remembering that very rocky time.

Usually, he, Bowie and the tots ate at the bar in the kitchen. Eating in the dining room again was kind of nice. Napkins and everything. And in the center of the square table, she'd set a pretty glass filled with Indian paintbrush. His mama had loved those red-orange wildflowers. Seeing them brought back good memories.

"Is the food okay?" Kyra asked anxiously, as if men who'd worked outside all day were particular. Especially men who'd been spared the task of cooking the meal. "I found the recipe on the blog of a rancher's wife, so I thought you might like it."

"Great," Wade said around a mouthful of ground beef, potatoes and cheese.

He squinted at his freshly filled fork. Were those chili beans? Or maybe kidney beans? Not too spicy for the toddlers. Tasty.

The trio of imps was making a royal mess of the food she'd put on each tray next to some sliced bell peppers. Even with plastic spoons in one hand, they mostly ate with their fingers.

She'd tried to make biscuits, which were as hard as his kneecap, but Wade gnawed through one anyway and shot a warning glance to Bowie to do the same. He didn't have the heart to tell her there was a bag of frozen biscuits and other quick items in the utility room Deepfreeze.

He snuck a look at the nanny, across from him, straight and proper in her chair, left hand in her lap unless she was feeding a baby. She'd positioned herself near the triplets and occasionally scooped bites into accepting mouths. Independent Ben shook his head and refused to let her feed him.

Wade knew he should be assisting, but Kyra appeared to be handling things. He wanted to watch her in action. Trusting a woman, especially a young pretty city woman, didn't come easy.

She'd filled him in on the triplets' afternoon and sounded as if they'd done okay. She even showed him some pictures she'd taken. He forgot to do that a lot, and they were growing so fast. She offered to text them to his phone and email.

She'd made a schedule, too, and started training the little ones to adhere to it. He wasn't sure about regimentation but figured a little organization wouldn't hurt them. Since Janey'd left, they were often up too late at night or slept too long in the afternoon because he was occupied with ranch work.

He frowned at his plate. Was he a lousy father? Did Kyra think that about him?

Bowie waved a fork to get his attention. "Bull five looks a little better after the vet was out yesterday."

Wade dragged his traitorous eyes from the pretty nanny. "What about that cow with the prolapse?"

"She's all right."

"Prolapse?" Kyra asked. "I've never heard that term."

He explained the condition. Her eyes widened, but she said nothing. She just turned to wipe Ben's messy face, a useless endeavor, Wade could tell her. There was no point in wiping up until they were finished.

Bowie reached for another rock-hard biscuit. He was either really hungry or really thoughtful. Or a little of both. "Her calf is trying to scour, though."

"Must not have gotten enough colostrum. Did you give it some electrolytes?"

"Yes, and moved him to barn three with his mama." Bowie poked another fork of meat and potatoes in his mouth.

"Think he'll make it?"

Bowie took a few seconds to chew and swallow. "Likely. He was still feisty. I'll check on him before bed."

"Do I dare ask the meaning of scour?" Kyra asked.

Both he and Bowie turned their heads to answer. "Diarrhea."

They went on talking about the cow and calf, then segued into mucking manure in barn four before the rains started and turned the lot into something neither of them wanted to consider. The stench was something akin to a dead coyote.

After a bit, Wade realized the new nanny was especially quiet. She'd started out the meal with pep and conversation, but now she'd gone silent and turned away, her side to him, her attention on the children. She'd barely touched her food.

"Everything okay, Kyra?"

Her head swiveled in his direction. "Fine."

She didn't look fine. "You look…green. Are you sick?"

Trying for a laugh, Kyra waved a hand. "I'm not accustomed to ranch talk. That's all."

Seriously? What had they said that could be the least bit upsetting?

Manure was a fact of life.

Realization moved through him.

Manure might be a fact of ranch life, but Kyra was a city girl.

And he'd do well to remember that.

Kyra chased Abby into the nursery, listening to her squeal with delight at what she clearly thought was a game of tag-and-tickle.

Rounding up all three for a bath proved to be a real challenge.

"Need some reinforcements?"

Kyra looked up into a pair of laughing blue eyes. Wade leaned against the nursery door frame, watching her.

Watching, as if still deciding her value as a nanny.

During dinner, he'd lapsed into gloomy silence. She'd thought he was upset because she'd found his table conversation unappetizing.

Now, he was smiling again.

Puzzling man.

"When I get two in the bathroom," she said, ignoring thoughts of the man, "the other one races back into the nursery."

"Yeah, they think it's a game." He pushed away from the door and stepped inside.

"I noticed." She caught the little girl and carried her into the bathroom where Caden sat on a rug, naked as the day he was born, chatting to a yellow rubber ducky. "That's two. Guard the door and I'll go after Benjamin."

Wade laughed. "I've got them."

On his haunches, he braced himself in front of the bathroom opening while she chased down a squealing Ben.

Somehow, they secured the trio inside the small room and got them into the bathtub, along with several tub toys.

Both adults knelt by the tub, shoulder to shoulder. Though she wielded a sponge to wash a protesting Ben, Kyra was acutely aware of the man at her side. He smelled of the outdoors, not the disgusting things they'd discussed at dinner.

With a mental shake, Kyra focused her attention on bath time.

Noticing Wade was…discomfiting.

"How did you ever manage this alone?" She soaped Abby's back and arms and dodged a splash from Ben. He chortled and splashed again.

"Bowie helped out," he said. "Sometimes. Once we get them in the tub, the rest is cake."

Abby grabbed for Caden's favorite ducky. Caden boo-hooed.

Wade rescued the situation by trading Abby a pink pig for the duck, all the while singing, "Rub-a-dub-dub, three kids in a tub."

"Cake for you," she said, bumping his side. "Rock-hard biscuits for me."

Wade's head turned. Twinkling blue eyes were so close she could see the yellow sunbursts around his pupils. "I didn't want to say anything."

"Kind of obvious, wasn't it?" She smiled into those eyes.

He smiled back.

She heard a *kerplunk* from somewhere. Hopefully,

not from her heart. A baby must have dropped a toy in the water.

Managing to turn her attention to the task of shampooing Abby's hair, she considered the last two days. She'd definitely misjudged Wade Trudeau. But even if he was a nice man, a good guy, she did not intend to fall for him.

A week later, Wade rode his horse beside Bowie's as they checked for a gap in the east fence. Some of their new baby calves had been loose on the county road this morning.

"Didn't you and Riley ride this fence line last week?"

"Yes," Bowie replied. "No gaps."

Wade squinted toward the east where the Sundown Ranch adjoined Keno land. "Think the Kenos had something to do with those calves getting out?"

"Maybe. But it's rained a lot this week, too."

Right. Rain sometimes washed gaps through the fences, especially near the creeks. Fence posts loosened in wet ground. "Let's ride the creek and check fence there."

They turned their horses in that direction. Moist earth squished beneath their horses' hooves. Green grass, thick and lush the way ranchers liked, had begun to spread across the pastures.

Pudge jogged alongside Wade's buckskin gelding, happy as a frog on a lily pad.

Bowie kept his countenance, quiet and watchful. The man could spot a deer two hundred yards away in tree-lined woods and could point out a squirrel thirty feet up in a sycamore.

Wade depended heavily on his cousin to find lost calves and cantankerous mama cows who wanted to hide their babies.

Bowie had an affinity with nature that Wade couldn't match. He was born to be a cowboy who spent his days in the great outdoors.

A hunter's eyes, that was what Dad had said about Bowie's uncanny abilities in the woods and fields.

Dad. Wade's heart pinched. He missed him, missed Mom and Trent. All gone too soon. Thoughts of Trent stabbed like an ice pick. His fault. His guilt to carry to his grave.

Would Yates ever forgive him and come home?

"There." Bowie pointed somewhere in the distance. "Fence down."

"Where?" Wade adjusted his hat against the sun and squinted. He saw nothing.

"Come on." Bowie clicked his tongue, and his bay mare picked up her pace.

Wade could do little else but follow.

They reached the five-strand barbed-wire fence they'd built across the creek to divide the Sundown Ranch from Keno property.

Bud Keno and his boys complained that the creek was completely on Keno land, though the abstract labeled the water source as belonging to the Sundown. To avoid trouble, Dad had built the fence right down the middle, dividing the wide creek in two, one section for each ranch.

Even that hadn't helped. Keno sabotaged the fence regularly. At least, Wade thought it was Keno. No one else had reason to.

As he dismounted, he growled low in his throat. This fence had been tight four days ago.

Bowie, on his haunches by the creek, looked up. "Could have been cut."

"Kenos." Wade reached in his saddlebag for fencing pliers and handed them to his cousin.

Could have been cut wasn't justification to ride over to the Keno house and cause trouble. Showing up on a doorstep with threats was Bud Keno's way of doing things, not his.

But he sure wanted to confront his less-than-friendly neighbors.

"Unless we know for certain a Keno is the culprit, nothing we can do."

Bowie nodded.

Butting heads with the Kenos was a full-time job if anyone wanted it. Neither Trudeau did. They put up with a lot to keep the peace. He didn't want any more deaths on his conscience.

But he wasn't paying Keno eight grand for nothing, either.

Lord, I hate this neighbor trouble. Turning the other cheek hasn't accomplished a thing.

"You mind finishing up here?" he asked.

"Why? You said you're not going to see Keno."

"I'm not."

A grin split Bowie's face. "The nanny?"

A hot flush burned up the back of Wade's neck. He rubbed at the spot. "Going to see my kids. Make sure they're okay. Kyra's new to caring for three toddlers. I don't know her that well. I gotta keep an eye on them."

"Uh-huh." Bowie grinned again, bigger this time. "You're keeping an eye on the nanny, too. I saw how you bumped her out of the way this morning and fixed breakfast so she could sip her coffee."

For a man who didn't talk much, Bowie was sure mouthy today.

"She looked tired. We don't want to run her off by overworking her."

"Seems like she's trying to prove something."

"I noticed." The new nanny had taken exactly two days to settle in before she'd taken charge of the house, the cabin, the babies. "She's not afraid of hard work."

"You like her."

Wade hiked a shoulder. "She's the person caring for my kids. If I didn't like her, she'd be gone."

"No, I mean, you *like* her. She's pretty and interesting." Bowie gave the loose fence post a jerk to straighten it. "Smells nice, too."

Wade pointed. "Don't go there, Bowie. You know my thoughts on women, especially girlie city types."

"Seems like Kyra's doing all right for herself out here in the boonies. No complaints so far." He twisted two wires together. "Right?"

Right. She was.

"But she's still a city girl." And a woman who would hightail it back to Tulsa at summer's end. Another reason to steer clear of her.

Except he couldn't. Not as long as she was the nanny. Which he hoped was forever.

Disgruntled at the turn of conversation and his own troubling thoughts, he tossed a leg over the buckskin and gathered the reins. "Meet you at barn one. Riley's setting up to work yearlings later today."

"Tell the nanny I said hello."

Wade gave him the death stare.

His cousin grinned.

Pudge climbed out of the creek and shook water on Bowie.

Wade laughed and rode away.

The air was sweet this afternoon with the fragrance of spring blooms and fresh air. Sunshine heated the back of his shirt. He loved this land, loved riding fence and wrangling cattle. Ranching was hard work, but he wouldn't trade it for any other life.

If he had, would Sabrina still be his wife?

Probably not. He'd never understood what made Sabrina happy. It sure wasn't him or those three little babies she'd left behind.

Like Yates, she'd simply left.

He couldn't understand how his brother could have walked away. Yates was the best cowboy, best rancher of the family. He understood weather patterns, could smell dirt and know what minerals needed to be added. He could birth a calf or a colt as well as any vet. And no one could match him on a horse.

Yet, Yates had simply gotten up one morning, tossed his duffel bag in his truck and driven away. Not a word of warning. He'd simply left and never returned.

The hurt of that gnawed inside Wade all the time. His fault, he supposed. He'd driven his brother from the ranch he loved.

He was good at driving people away. Yates. Sabrina.

Wade wiped a hand across his eyes and mentally closed the door on his negative thoughts. God had blessed him with a beautiful spring day, a fine ranch and three children he would die for.

That should be enough.

Fifteen minutes later, he rode the path toward barn one, which put him in eyeshot of the house. He hadn't intended to stop. Not after Bowie's wise cracks.

His insides lifted at the sight on his back lawn.

On a quilt in the sunshine, Kyra played with the triplets.

The sun reflected the gold and copper in her hair. She wore it down today, tucked behind her ears, a curved sweep along her shoulders.

She had real pretty hair.

The triplets toddled around her, doing what toddlers do, which made no sense to an adult but was fun for them.

He slowed Doc to watch a minute. His babies were okay. No need to stop.

Then Kyra saw him and waved. She said something to the little ones and pointed toward him. She lifted Caden's hand in a baby wave that tickled Wade's chest. The other two joined forces with waves of their own, then started toward him, yelling at the top of their lungs.

He loved when they ran to him, as if he were the most important person on earth.

But Kyra caught them and dragged them back onto the quilt.

What could a man do? Riding past would be rude. His children would be disappointed.

Nudging Doc with his knees, he turned the horse from the trail. As he approached, Kyra's eyes widened. Caden sat in her lap, the constant cuddler, but she grabbed the other two and pulled them as close to her as she could, as if shielding them.

They looked real cute, a pile of babies and a pretty woman.

When he and Doc were ten feet from the edge of the quilt, she put out a stop-sign hand. "Don't come any closer."

He hadn't intended to, but there was anxiety in her voice.

City girl, he thought, recalling his conversation with Bowie. He wouldn't endanger his babies around a horse. Didn't she know that?

Wade pulled the buckskin to a stop and dismounted. Leaving Doc ground tied, he joined the foursome.

He eased down on the quilt. Benjamin whacked him

with Caden's favorite rubber duck. Wade took the toy and danced it up Ben's belly until the baby grabbed for it and fell backward, chuckling.

"My favorite sound in the world," Kyra said.

His, too.

"How's your day going?" he asked, for lack of anything smarter to say.

"As you can see, so far so good. I managed to get all three of them fed, diapered and dressed without major incident. And—" she held up one finger "—finished two loads of laundry. I feel like a domestic princess."

She laughed, and so he did, too. All the while, he wondered why the idea of her laundering his shirts was so much more appealing than when Janey had done the wash.

They talked of mundane things. He told her about the cut fence and a little about their unfriendly neighbors. She told him about her pastor dad and talked about her best friend, Amy.

Wade worried she'd miss them too much and run back to Tulsa. He told her to invite them for a visit.

She smiled a lot, and he liked that about her. Her humor, her can-do attitude, her tenderness with the babies. There was a lot to appreciate about his nanny.

Maybe he was starting to trust her a little more than he'd let on to Bowie.

Truth was he liked the nanny. He liked her company. Having a woman on the ranch brightened up the days.

He didn't ponder the reasons.

Caden remained in her lap, soaking up her tender attention. Abby and Ben chased each other in circles, giggling. Occasionally, one of them ran to him or to Kyra. They'd taken to her as if she'd always been here.

Wade didn't want to think about her leaving them, breaking their little hearts.

As an adult, he could keep his emotions in check. They were innocent babies.

But what choice did he have? Kyra was here. He needed her. The triplets needed her. Sundown Valley's employment service was still searching for a grandmotherly nanny to replace Kyra in September. So far, nothing.

"Why the frown?" Her soft voice pulled his gaze to her face.

"Aw, nothing." He plucked a weed and tickled Abby's cheek, tempted to tickle Kyra's sandaled foot, too.

He resisted. Barely.

The sunshine and the butterflies kissing the wildflowers on his lawn made him lazy. A cardinal fluttered to the grass under a tall sycamore.

Wade pointed. "There's your bird."

She'd told him of her love for the scarlet birds, how they reminded her of her mother. Now, whenever he spotted a cardinal, he thought of his own lost loved ones.

Kyra, with Caden patting her leg with his ducky, watched the bird until it flew away, her expression tranquil.

She carried that air of tranquility with her even in the chaos of triplets.

Wade peered toward the barn. From here, he could see clearly. Riley's truck wasn't there yet.

Five more minutes with his family wouldn't ruin his workday.

When Abby ran to him with a flower she'd plucked and was about to eat, he took the weed, and to stave off protests, lifted her high above his head and flew her like an airplane.

This activated both boys, who tackled him. He gladly fell onto his back on the quilt and gently wrestled the trio of delights.

"Oh, I forgot to tell you," Kyra said, as Abby poked him in the eye.

Kyra rescued him by pulling Abby slightly away. Her fingers brushed his shoulder. The touch buzzed through his veins, pleasant. Her soft perfume drifted around his head.

Lazily, he rotated his head toward her, enjoying the sound of her voice, the movement of her gloss-shined lips.

Attraction. He'd almost forgotten how good it could feel.

Not that he'd do anything except enjoy feeling human again.

"The area rug was delivered today," she was saying, "and it's perfect. The babies helped me put it down."

His mouth twitched. "I bet they did."

The large rectangular rug was the final thing she'd ordered for the bunkhouse. His wallet was glad the shopping was over.

"You'll have to come out to the cabin and see how everything looks when I get finished."

"Sure." Spend more time with Kyra after the triplets were in bed? Why not? The more he knew about her, the more comfortable he'd be with her as the triplets' nanny.

He was all about the babies. Being attracted to the nanny had nothing to do with it.

"I want to talk to you about something else, too." She sounded serious.

Wade's pulse thumped. He extricated himself from a trio of miniature bodies and sat up. "You're not quitting, are you?"

Caden toddled to Kyra and climbed into her lap. She kissed the top of his barely-there brown hair.

Oh, man. Her tenderness melted him.

"No, I'm not quitting. A deal is a deal, where I come from." She paused to wipe grass from Ben's outstretched hand. "I was thinking about going into Sundown Valley to shop for curtains and a few other items."

So much for his wallet. His shoulder jerked. "Go."

"Three car seats won't fit in my car."

He snorted, then staved off Ben's finger attack to his nostrils. "I doubt if even one sack of groceries will fit in that little toy you drive."

She wrinkled her nose at him. "I don't mind taking the triplets. Since you have a triple stroller, I might take them to a park to play. They're big enough to enjoy the kiddie toys."

The babies would love playing in the park. Not one of them had ever been on a slide or a swing. Was he neglectful for not taking them?

He glanced at the expansive backyard. Maybe he should buy a swing set. Were they big enough for such a thing?

"Take my truck." He motioned in the general direction of the garage. "The baby seats are already installed."

"Are you sure you don't mind?"

"You can drive a stick shift, can't you?"

Her face fell. "Your truck has a manual shifter?"

He laughed. "Naw. I was teasing. Just wanted to see your reaction." He poked her foot with the tip of his boot. "City girl."

She whacked his arm. He rubbed it, grinning. "You punch like a city girl, too."

She made that cute face again and he was tempted to hug her.

He hugged Ben instead. Ben wiggled free and bumped into Abby, who fell to her padded bottom and began to cry.

"Hey now, you're okay." Wade lifted Abby to her feet, distracting her with a toy.

Sound and movement came from the area near the barn. Riley had arrived.

"Break's over." Untangling himself from the kids, Wade stood to his feet. "Gotta go. The truck keys are hanging on the rack inside the garage door. Use it anytime."

"Thank you. That's thoughtful of you."

There she went again, telling him he was thoughtful. If she didn't stop, he'd start to believe her.

Sabrina had called him a self-centered jerk. He hadn't meant to be. He'd tried to please her. Had he succeeded for even one day?

Looking into Kyra's warm eyes, seeing her smile and her easy way with the triplets made him wonder if *she* was happy here on the ranch. She seemed content, didn't complain, but was she happy? Had he done enough to see to her comfort, to make her want to stay? Hopefully longer than September, though for now, he kept that wish to himself.

He took three steps toward Doc, then pivoted around. "Say, I was thinking. Other than the weekends, you don't get much free time. Would you like to ride with me sometime? The ranch is beautiful in the spring of the year. The mountains are in bloom, trees budding." She claimed to love the mountains. "Bowie could watch the triplets."

Her eyes widened. "Ride? As in, ride a horse?"

Her reaction, much like the moment when he'd ridden closer than she liked, gave him pause.

"You're not afraid of horses, are you? This is a ranch. You can't possibly be afraid of horses."

"Not afraid, exactly." She opened a zippy bag and handed Caden a blueberry. "I've never actually been around a horse. They're big. And intimidating."

The woman was afraid of horses. His life and livelihood were in the saddle. His triplets would learn to ride before their feet could reach the stirrups.

"What about cows? Do they scare you, too?"

"Well," she hedged, sheepish now, as she handed out more berries to the tots. "I once touched a baby cow at the Tulsa State Fair." Shoulders hunching, she pulled a cute face. "That was a long time ago."

A baby cow.

"A calf. You touched a calf." He shook his head and laughed. "You really are a city girl."

She laughed, too, that warm sparkly sound that made him think crazy thoughts. "Guilty to the tip of my pedicured toes."

She lifted a sandaled foot and wiggled those toes, the purple nail polish gleaming in the sun.

"I like animals, but I'm not accustomed to the big ones. I grew up with goldfish and small dogs."

As if Pudge understood the reference to his species, he rose from his spot in the shade along the back of the house and trotted over. Kyra rubbed a hand down his speckled back.

Ben toddled near to pat the affable dog's face. Pudge gave the baby's head a swipe of his pink tongue.

"Spending time with a good horse would get you used to their size," Wade said, "and all our horses are dead broke. They have to be to work a ranch. I'll teach you to ride if you're interested."

The more he thought about it, the better he liked the

idea. She'd enjoy riding a horse once she learned. Then they could ride together, maybe go fishing or take a picnic. If he bought one of those safety carrier things, they could even take the babies. He wanted to teach his kids the pleasure of horses as soon as possible. He hadn't had the time or the help. Until now. Now would be the perfect beginning.

"Thank you, Wade, but I don't think I'll be here long enough for riding lessons."

His mood plummeted. What was he thinking? That if he taught her to ride a horse she'd suddenly love living two hours from the nearest city and want to stay on the Sundown beyond the summer?

Yes, that was exactly what he'd thought.

Dumb.

"Got it." With a single short nod, he headed for his horse and the barn.

When would he ever learn?

Chapter Six

The Sundown Valley Physician's Clinic boasted eight permanent doctors, a surgeon and several weekly specialists.

Kyra and Wade waited inside an exam room for Dr. Edgerton, the town's pediatrician, to examine the triplets. Today was their well-baby visit.

The fact that Wade had come along told Kyra one of two things. Either he was a great dad who wanted total involvement in the life of his children, or he didn't trust the nanny to do this by herself.

She opted to believe the first, having long since decided that Wade was a better father than she'd initially assumed.

"Nineteen pounds," the nurse declared as she lifted Abby into Kyra's waiting arms. "Here you go, Mommy."

"Oh, no, I'm not their mother." A blush rushed up Kyra's neck. "I'm their nanny."

The nurse looked from her to Wade. "Sorry. I'm new. I just assumed—"

Kyra waved off the apology. "That's okay."

Wade made no comment about the mistake, but something in his expression had darkened, as if the idea of a mother for his triplets gave him indigestion.

Was it because of his ex?

Without a glance at her, Wade rose to hold Benjamin

on the scales while the nurse took the reading and then did the same with Caden.

Both boys outweighed their sister, but not by much.

"Is that normal for their ages?" Wade asked as Dr. Edgerton entered the room.

The doctor glanced at the notes the nurse jotted, her white coat swinging open to reveal a sunny yellow belted dress. "Normal for triplets."

She shook Wade's hand and then introduced herself to Kyra.

Blond, attractive and friendly, the young doctor exuded an easy, confident bedside manner that engendered trust. Kyra liked her right away.

"Let's have a look at these adorable little ones."

Kyra and Wade took turns holding a baby while the doctor executed a very thorough exam. She asked question after question. Eat and sleep habits, developmental milestones, behaviors and more.

Wade answered most questions, although Kyra knew a few things about the babies' latest food preferences, a fact that earned appreciative looks from the rancher dad.

She preened a little, pleased. Ben and Abby spoke a few comprehensible words, although someone who didn't know them probably wouldn't understand. Caden was the only who didn't seem ready to talk. He'd rather snuggle.

"Is Caden okay, Doc?" Worry creased Wade's forehead. "Shouldn't he be picking up a few words by now, too?"

Dr. Edgerton patted Caden's arm. "You're doing great, little man. No worries." To Wade, she said, "Every baby is different. He has plenty of time before we'd be concerned. From what I see, our man Caden is a listener, and that's perfectly normal, especially in multiples."

She studied her computer tablet. "Looks like today is another vaccine day. Time for a DTaP booster."

Kyra shot an uneasy glance toward Wade. "This is a first for me. I'm glad you're here."

Truthfully, she was glad for the rancher's company anytime. And not only because he helped her with the children.

Wade grimaced. "I have to admit I don't like this part, but I'm an old hand by now."

She raised her eyebrows. "Bet you'd rather vaccinate calves."

He pointed. "Got that right."

The babies proved to be troupers. Only Ben cried, and Wade walked the small space with him, patting and soothing. The sight splashed in the center of Kyra's heart, a drop of something as pure and precious as the love the cowboy had for his son.

When Abby's turn came, she puckered, her cute little lip quivering, but Kyra snuggled her close and pushed the button on a talking toy cell phone to distract her.

The doctor held Caden who was too occupied with the stethoscope around her neck to even notice when the skillful nurse slid the needle into his chubby thigh.

"All finished," the doctor said and placed Caden into the triple stroller before turning to Wade. "They're doing really well, Wade. Meeting milestones, catching up to their peers, very healthy triplets. I know this past year hasn't been easy for you, but whatever you're doing, keep it up."

Dr. Edgerton's veiled reference to his single-dad status inflamed Kyra's curiosity. What had happened to the babies' mother? Why had she left? And when? Had Wade been the only parent since birth? Did the doctor know?

The cowboy clearly had no intention of discussing his personal life in front of her.

Instead, he hitched his chin toward Kyra. "They have a good nanny."

At the compliment, Kyra's pulse fluttered, a silly reaction.

"I see that." The doctor smiled, her gaze moving between Wade and Kyra with a curious expression.

Did she think there was something personal going on between Kyra and Wade?

Did Kyra want there to be?

Her eyes slid toward the rancher. Yes, she liked him. Yes, he was handsome. And maybe she'd like to spend more time with him as a man and a woman, and not always as nanny and boss.

But he'd vehemently dealt with that complication before he'd hired her as nanny.

Wade had been burned. His full focus was the ranch and his family. Women were at the bottom of his favorites list.

Except they weren't. Not really. Even if he didn't trust her much, he seemed to like her. He'd even offered to teach her horseback riding.

Fighting a blush, she tuned back to the pediatrician.

"Unless a problem arises," Dr. Edgerton was saying, "I won't need to see them again until sometime around their second birthday."

"Sounds good." Wade shook her extended hand. "Sounds great, actually."

"A pleasure to meet you, Kyra. Take care of Wade and these little ones. He's needed someone like you." With that curious statement, the doctor left the exam room.

Take care of Wade as well as the triplets? What exactly had the doctor meant by that?

While the implications rolled round and round in her head, Kyra settled the triplets in the three-way stroller. With Wade in front holding doors, Kyra rolled through each one and headed toward the parking lot.

Wade snicked the truck locks and opened the back door. "This calls for a celebration."

Kyra unbuckled the triplets and handed Abby to her dad. "It does?"

"Certainly. We came out of shot duty relatively unscathed. Only one baby cried, and he didn't cry very long. *I* cry longer than that!"

Kyra laughed at his silliness.

They completed the baby relay, and with the trio settled and buckled, Kyra rounded the truck to the passenger side.

Wade followed.

She might be an independent woman, but she appreciated a man with manners.

He opened her door, but she didn't get inside. Instead, she turned to face him. "So what do you suggest in the way of celebration?"

With the sun gleaming off the truck and the afternoon stretched out before them, he leaned his strong rancher's arm along the door frame, relaxed and easy and so close that she could feel the warmth of his body.

"How about ice cream?" His eyes glowed with something that made her pulse skitter. Again.

"Sounds perfect." The words came out soft, breathy.

Kyra clamped down on her back molars.

What was wrong with her today?

"Great." Wade popped a hand against the side of the truck and stepped back.

Befuddled, Kyra climbed into the high cab, intensely aware of the rancher's fingers supporting her back.

Her muscles ached today as they did most days. Wade didn't know, but his touch felt nice. Really nice.

Some emotion, anticipation perhaps, though she didn't know what for, hovered in the cab as Wade drove to an ice cream shop at one end of Main Street. The Scoop, a cute place with inside seating and three sidewalk tables, was busy. Customers came and went with a variety of ice-cream delights or fountain drinks.

After getting their orders from a teenage clerk who obviously had a crush on the handsome rancher, they opted for a table in the pleasant sunshine.

Wade greeted several people he knew—a perk, she supposed, of small-town living. She received more than one speculative glance, though Wade identified her to each of his friends as nanny to the triplets.

The questioning looks stirred unwanted emotions in Kyra. Husband, babies, home. She desired those things.

Someday. In God's timing.

Kyra turned her focus to feeding the triplets. Three little bird mouths demanding ice cream took her mind off her attractive companion. A little.

Ignoring Wade wasn't easy.

He was fun and outgoing, not at all the rattled cowboy she'd first met.

During the well-baby visit and now a stop for ice cream, a family feeling had sprung up around Kyra like crabgrass. She needed to weed it out. So far, she hadn't.

"Wade Trudeau! You old hermit you." An attractive blonde in a turquoise sundress rushed to their table. "Where have you been hiding?"

The woman with her, a brunette in shorts and a T-shirt, went straight for the babies. "Oh, these adorable triplets. Wade, they're so cute."

"They're all going to have your gorgeous blue eyes,

aren't they?" The blonde beamed at Wade with such obvious admiration Kyra had to close her eyes to keep from rolling them.

Wade appeared oblivious.

"Kyra," he said, "meet Shawna and Becky. They attend church at North Cross."

"Your church?" she asked.

"Yes."

"You should join us, Kyra." The brunette, Becky, tossed her long hair behind her back. Tall and strong-looking, with legs that went on forever, she had lovely brown skin and Native American features. "North Cross is a great church."

"Weekends are Kyra's time off," Wade said. "She's not here."

"I drive back to Tulsa on Friday night," Kyra explained. "My dad is a pastor there."

"What about our Bible study group that meets on Tuesday nights? We'd love to have you. Seven o'clock. Fellowship hall."

"I think I would enjoy that." Kyra figured if she was going to be in the Sundown Valley area for an entire summer, she'd like to make some friends outside the ranch. Though she and Amy talked or texted every day, Kyra missed the in-person interaction.

"Maybe you could arm-wrestle this guy into coming again." Shawna jerked a thumb toward Wade and winked, whether at him or her, Kyra didn't know. "At one time, he never missed."

"That was before I had three kids who are generally in bed by seven." Wade scooped a spoonful of ice cream into Ben's open mouth. The little guy pounded the stroller with both hands and drooled melted ice cream, his expression delighted.

"You never know. Something might work out. Your cousin, Bowie, rarely misses." Shawna waggled her eyebrows and waved a hand in front of her face. Apparently, she thought Bowie was a hottie, too.

Wade laughed. "My cousin's a catch, huh? I'll tell him you said so."

Shawna stuck a finger in his face. "Don't you dare, Wade Trudeau. He already avoids me."

"Probably because he thinks you're pretty."

"He does?" She perked up.

Becky gave her friend a gentle shove. "Shawna. Seriously. We have to go before you make a fool of yourself."

"Too late!" Shawna hunched her shoulders and giggled. "But we do have to go. Wade, are you bringing these adorables to the Spring Fling next Saturday?"

"Maybe. Depends on their mood and my workload."

"Try hard. And bring your cousin, too." Shawna turned toward Kyra. "See you at Bible study Tuesday night. Okay?"

"I'll plan on it. Thank you."

As the friendly pair departed, Kyra took out her phone and typed the Bible study information in the notes.

"Nice women." She stuck her phone in her pocket. Caden reached his arms toward her, indicating he wanted up.

Without a second thought, she unbuckled and lifted him from the stroller.

"Yeah." Wade didn't seem too enthused now that the women were gone.

"Is there something I should know about them? You look a little…put off. Should I avoid their friendship?"

"They're both terrific Christians. I've known them all my life."

"Then what's the hesitation?"

He didn't meet her gaze. Instead, he wiped Ben's face with a paper napkin and murmured, "None at all."

But she hadn't imagined the change in attitude. What was the deal?

Days later, Wade was still rehashing his negative reaction to Shawna and Becky inviting Kyra to Bible study. He felt like a jerk. They were great gals, which was exactly the problem. He didn't want his friends hurt again.

Frankly, after his ex-wife's behavior, he was amazed they'd reached out to Kyra at all.

In Sabrina's view, Shawna, Becky and the other Sundown Valley locals were backwoods hillbillies. She'd quickly cold-shouldered them, claiming they had nothing in common. Then she'd complained of loneliness and boredom.

He, as he'd discovered not long after their honeymoon to the Virgin Islands, was boring. Ranch life was boring. All he did was work. She needed action, fun, shopping!

Most days he wondered why she'd married him in the first place.

He also wondered if his bitterness toward Sabrina was clouding his judgment.

Kyra had given him no reason to suspect she was a snob.

But then neither had Sabrina at first. She'd wanted a cowboy. Trouble was, her idea of the cowboy life didn't include the hard truth that cowboys weren't only shiny belt buckles and Stetson hats. They worked outside with animals. They sweat. They got dirty. They tracked unmentionable things on the floors.

City folk didn't have a clue.

Kyra's soft voice dispelled his troubled thoughts. "They're going to love this, Wade."

He glanced up from the outdoor swing set they were

putting together while the babies napped. The nanny looked cute sitting cross-legged on the grass in capris and sandals, the assembly diagram he hadn't bothered to read spread out before her. The baby monitor rested on the grass beside her.

Would Sabrina have read the directions aloud to him? Would she have patiently helped him sort the chunky plastic nuts and bolts and assemble the heavy-duty apparatus? He didn't think so.

Which elevated his opinion of this particular city girl.

"It's supposed to grow with them until they start kindergarten." He grimaced. "*If* I can get it put together before then."

She laughed, and her nose wrinkled in that cute way he always seemed to notice.

"We got this, Trudeau." She flexed a biceps. "Stay strong."

When she said things like that, he forgot all about his ex-wife.

"The slide goes on next."

He frowned at the structure. One side listed to the west, the other to the south. "You sure?"

"Let me look again." With a concentration frown tugging her eyebrows together, she caught her bottom lip between her teeth. "Yes. Now that the main frame is attached over the top, the slide connects to the end of that, then the ladder on the side and the swings last."

She rose from the grass and brought the paper instructions to him. "See?"

In his effort to do exactly that, he moved closer to peer over her shoulder. Kyra's upper arm grazed his chest. His chin hovered directly over her beautiful hair. Her perfume circled around them until he could barely focus on the diagram. Fact of the matter, his eyes might have crossed a little.

She put her finger on a drawing and tilted her face toward his. "Right there."

Wade stared down into her eyes. She stared back. Something flickered in her hazel irises. Something flickered inside him, too, as if a switch had turned on.

His chest tightened. Confusion muddled his brain.

He was a grown man with three kids and a big ranch to run. Why did he suddenly lose the ability to reason whenever Kyra got too close? He wasn't a teenager. He most certainly knew better than to allow testosterone to override his common sense. Been there, done that and had plenty of scars and three motherless babies to show for it.

With the willpower that made him a successful rancher, he blinked and diverted his gaze to the diagram.

His heart, however, continued to ricochet against his rib cage.

Wade cleared his throat and, breaking the physical contact that was driving him a little crazy, he stepped back to the almost-completed swing set. "Got it. Slide first."

Obviously not as bothered by the strange moment as he'd been, Kyra pointed to something behind him. "Who's that?"

Wade pivoted. Dust rose over the long driveway leading into the Sundown. "You expecting anyone? Or any more deliveries?"

"No."

An irrational, hopeful thought shot adrenaline into his brain. Had Yates come home?

In moments, an older red pickup truck came into sight.

Wade's hopes crashed and died. Not only was the visitor not his long-lost brother, he was someone Wade would prefer never to see again.

The red truck braked to a gravel-grinding stop thirty yards from where Wade and Kyra stood.

A beefy red-faced man in a gray Stetson and dusty boots bolted from the truck and charged across the lawn like a mad bull. His tree-trunk legs chewed up the space between them faster than Wade thought possible.

Wade braced for the inevitable barrage of cursing, berating and threats.

With his eyes on the advancing man, he spoke quietly to Kyra. "Go in the house."

He felt her bristle, but she made no move to follow his directive.

He spun toward her and, between gritted teeth, growled the word, "Go!"

The last thing he wanted was for Kyra to witness Bud Keno's ugly behavior.

She sucked in a quick gasp and glared at him before stalking toward the back porch.

Wade whipped around to face his ever-angry neighbor. "What do you want now, Keno? Wasn't cutting our fence enough mischief for this month?"

"I don't know what you're talking about. You're the one up to no good, and me and my boys are sick of it. I come to collect my money."

"Then you've wasted your time and mine. We don't owe you a dime."

Keno let out a virulent streak of profanity. Wade whispered a silent prayer of thanks that Kyra had gone inside.

Keno leaned in, his eyes bulging. Sweat glistened on his red face. "You'll pay one way or the other, Trudeau. Better keep that in mind."

"Exactly what are you trying to say?" Wade's hands fisted at his sides. "Are you threatening me?"

"Call it what you want. I gave you fair warning weeks ago when I brought over the bill for all them calves you cost me. You ignored me then. You won't ignore me now."

Wade sucked in a deep breath and blew it out, praying

for calm and for the right words to diffuse a volatile man who seemed intent on continuing an ancient family feud.

"Look, Bud, let's be reasonable and talk this out without swearing or accusations. I don't appreciate you using the Lord's name like that."

"The time for talk is over." Keno shoved an envelope into Wade's hands. "We're suing. And if you or any of your thieving bunch step foot on my land again, you better have your will up to date."

The warning was too clear and too dangerous to be ignored. Wade knew Kenos hated Trudeaus and had for generations, but this was taking things too far. "Don't be tossing out threats like that."

"No threat. Fact. I'll see you in court."

Keno spun on his boots and stomped back to his truck.

Wade shoved the envelope in his back pocket and rubbed both hands over his face. The action did nothing to dispel his burning frustration.

What had been a very nice afternoon erecting the babies' play set with Kyra had turned ugly.

The swing set would have to wait. He had to call a lawyer.

With a groan, Wade turned toward the house.

There on the back porch, her eyes wide and worried, stood Kyra.

Adrenaline, already at stratospheric levels, jacked a fresh dose into his blood stream.

"I told you to go inside!" Wade shouted as he stormed across the grass.

With every step, Keno's dratted envelope poked out of his pocket and into the small of his back, fueling his irritation.

"I'm a grown woman, Wade, and I did not appreciate your tone." She sounded calm and reasonable, something he wasn't.

His boots scraped as he stepped up on the porch. "My tone and my order to get in the house were for your protection."

"Your *order*?" She stretched to her full height, suddenly not so calm. "You may be my employer, *Mister* Trudeau, but this isn't the fifteenth century, and I resent being ordered to do anything."

Didn't she understand? He didn't want anyone hurt. Not again. Not on his watch. And Keno was far from stable.

If Wade had to make Kyra mad to shield her from Keno, he would. Fact of the business, he'd do whatever necessary to protect her and his triplets.

"Your job is to watch the babies. *They* need protecting even if you think you don't."

"I'm perfectly aware of that, and they are fine. Every single one of them is asleep." She shoved the monitor under his nose. "See for yourself."

Sure enough, all three of his dumplings, bottoms in the air, slept in their cribs. Two faces turned toward the camera. The third turned away.

Some of his aggravation seeped away. He groaned and let his head drop backward. "Right. Okay. Let it go. But steer clear of Bud Keno and his boys. You understand?"

Before she could shoot a retort guaranteed to burn his ears off, he pushed his hat down on his head and stalked off toward the barn.

Chapter Seven

"What burr got under your saddle?"

At his cousin's calmly asked question, Wade dropped the mama cow's foot he'd been doctoring and gave her backside a shove to send her out of the chute.

This scalding afternoon, he, Bowie and Riley were working the cattle from pasture four. Riley rounded them into the holding pen, Bowie guided them down the narrow metal alley, inspecting each one as they moved, and Wade did the doctoring in the squeeze chute. The blue heeler did his part, too, chasing down strays and keeping mad mamas at bay.

"Bud Keno paid us a little uninvited visit."

"Ah." Bowie, with Pudge's assistance, guided the next animal into the squeeze chute. She mooed at him but accepted her lot in life when Wade lowered the head gate, trapping her inside.

"He's suing us."

"No way." Bowie shoved the brim of his hat back, blinking like a hoot owl. "What for?"

"A lot of money." Wade accepted the loaded applicator gun Bowie handed his way. The two of them had done this job for so long they anticipated the other's next move. "If Keno and his never-ending complaints aren't bad enough, Kyra's mad at me."

"What did you do?"

"Nothing." He'd never understand women. Never. "I

told her to go in the house. She didn't. Then she was mad at me about it."

Bowie's soft laugh meandered above the sound of cattle banging against metal panels. A barn lot was a noisy place. Stinky, too, but the Trudeau boys were immune to the manure and muck stench.

"As little as I know about women, Wade, my man, I know better than that. Women don't like being bossed around."

Wade wrestled the cow's mouth open and injected the thick wormer paste. When she slung her head, fighting the head gate, he released the lever and let her run. She took off bucking and bawling into the hot afternoon. Dust swirled in her wake.

"Yeah," he admitted, "I might have been a little on the cranky side, too." Bud Keno could fire him up faster than a blowtorch on gasoline.

Bowie grunted as he pushed the next cow into place. "Not good, cuz."

"I was trying to get her away from Keno. The maniac came roaring up, loaded for bear, cussing a blue streak. Kyra's a nice woman, Bowie. Her daddy's a preacher! I can't allow her to hear the stuff that comes out of Bud Keno's nasty mouth."

"You can't allow it? Do you hear yourself, Wade?" A slow grin crept up his cousin's dark face. Black eyes sparkled. "You got it bad, son."

Wade grabbed for the next bovine head, wrestled its mouth open and filled its tongue with the pasty medication. "What are you talking about?"

"You. And the pretty nanny with the sweet nature who also happens to love your kids." Over his left chest, Bowie formed the fingers of both hands into a heart.

Wade turned a glare guaranteed to melt cement on his cousin.

"You've been out in the sun too long. You're going loco." But Wade's pulse took off faster than a racehorse in the Kentucky Derby.

Bowie smirked. The scoundrel actually smirked. "I call 'em as I see 'em."

"Huh. Better call the doc, get some glasses."

"You're saying I'm wrong?"

"That's right. You're wrong." He snarled at the tangled words. Words as tangled as his brain.

"Then you won't mind if I ask her out."

"Not happening, pal." Bowie might be joking, but the idea infuriated Wade. "I don't want a bunch of heathen cowhands scaring off my nanny. Including you."

Bowie's snicker was low and knowing. He had a way of saying a lot more with a look or a laugh than he did with words.

Today, he was full of talk. Talk that didn't make a lick of sense.

"Whatever you did wrong," the blabbermouth went on, "you'd better lope on in the house to kiss and make up. We need her. She cooks good and smells nice." He pointed a gloved finger. "And loves those babies. If Kyra quits because of your bad moods, I'm quitting, too."

Wade scoffed. "You can't quit. You're a partner."

His cousin answered with a lifted shoulder.

Bowie was right about one thing, doggone it. They needed Kyra in a bad way. They had neither the time nor the energy to juggle ranch work and three little ones again.

He'd have to find a way to smooth things over with the nanny.

Mulling over the situation, Wade paid little attention to either Bowie or Riley as they worked and talked. Rather, Riley talked and Bowie listened, laughing now and then to keep the conversation flowing. Riley was full of escapades and wild stories, most of them only half-true.

Riley wasn't a liar. But he often saw things a lot bigger than most other people.

By the time the barn work was finished and Wade had scrubbed his sweaty face and hands in the barn sink, he had an idea.

While the other two men headed off on tractors to separate pastures to cut hay, Wade decided to take a little break and drop in on his munchkins. And Kyra.

He spent the time praying as he walked the short distance across the open field toward the house. Praying had a way of setting his head straight.

A stand of wildflowers caught his eye, like the red-orange of a sunset against the green grass. Kyra liked sunsets. She liked flowers, too. The bunkhouse was filled with pots and jars full of plants.

Bowie's teasing weighed on him. Both the ridiculous romantic talk and the worry that she might up and quit on them.

Wade couldn't let that happen. He tried not to contemplate his cousin's other remarks. Falling for the nanny was out of the question. He needed her too badly as an employee. If he gave any hint of finding her attractive, she might run for the hills.

But that was the trouble—Kyra *was* attractive. Even Bowie, who ignored women better than any man Wade had ever known, wanted to take her out.

Maybe he'd been kidding. But what if he hadn't been?

With all these worries rattling around his head, Wade's mind wandered. Thinking, praying, he turned his gaze to the magnificent purple hills. Kyra loved the hills and mountains around Sundown Ranch. Claimed she liked to hike and camp. She'd even quoted one of his favorite

Bible verses to him. The one about looking to the mountains for help because God lived there.

Man, he liked the thought of that. God living right up on that big hilltop, watching out for him, never even taking a nap.

There was something incredibly reassuring in knowing an omniscient, omnipresent God was always there for him. Always.

Without the Lord Jesus this past year and a half, he'd have been a worse wreck than he'd been the day he hired Kyra.

She'd been God's answer to a desperate prayer.

Maybe he should take her hiking or on a wilderness picnic. Get her out of the house for a change, entertain her. Make sure she didn't get bored or restless.

Someday.

If she felt at home here on the Sundown, she might want to stay longer than the summer. The Kiamichi were beautiful in the fall and the destination of one of Oklahoma's best-kept secrets. Had she been here when the leaves changed and the mountains flamed with sunset colors?

Not knowing if the littles were napping, Wade entered the back door as quietly as possible. Kyra had created a schedule, but he didn't recall the babies' nap time.

The house was quiet. The only time that occurred was when the babies slept.

Taking off his boots, he grimaced at the muck he'd tracked in on what appeared to be freshly mopped tile. He should have shucked the footwear at the door.

Kyra was already mad. No use adding fuel to the flame. He grabbed a broom and dustpan and cleaned up his mess.

The house remained quiet. A beautiful sound.

Tiptoeing down the hall, he paused in the nursery's open doorway. Two babies still slept in their cribs. In the rocking chair, Kyra rocked Ben, his body angled across hers, his head on her shoulder.

Kyra didn't notice him at first, so Wade remained silent, observing for a bit as she stroked Benjamin's hair and made soft shushing sounds.

Wade no longer watched to be sure she was doing a good job. He watched because he was mesmerized.

The woman. The child. Madonna-like beauty.

A wave of tenderness moved through him, strong and mushy at the same time. This was the way things were supposed to be.

At times like these, when he watched Kyra with his triplets, he didn't see a nanny. He saw a loving mother.

And the thoughts scared him worse than being chased by a dozen Brahma bulls.

Kyra rocked and soothed the fussy baby, praying that the painful teething would soon subside. Baby drool pooled on the shoulder of her blouse. Benjamin was restless and miserable and only slept when she held him. The mood was uncharacteristic for bold, independent Ben. Her precious little Ben.

She'd fallen hard for these babies. Though they exhausted her every single day and left her with an aching back, she loved them.

She was growing fond of the men of Sundown Ranch, as well. Quiet Bowie with his pithy, wry humor had become a friend. He was a good listener, a gentle, artistic soul devoted to this ranch and his cousin. In his free time, he created gorgeous leatherwork in his shop.

Often in the evenings, he'd jump in his truck and leave the ranch. From Wade, she'd learned that Bowie was Sundown Valley's go-to guy. Anyone who needed a helping hand called on Bowie Trudeau and he rushed to the rescue.

She didn't see much of Riley, who drove to the ranch from Sundown Valley each day, but he was always willing to move a piece of furniture or unload boxes for her.

Then there was Wade. Her feelings were all over the place about that particular cowboy. He was not at all the person she'd first thought him to be. Intelligent and well-read, Wade was absolutely dedicated to his ranch and his little family. Most importantly, he loved the Lord.

She liked him. Most of the time, she enjoyed being with him.

Except for the fact that he made her pulse flutter. Not only when he came too close, but every time they crossed paths, or even when she smelled the faintest hint of his deep woodsy aftershave. She even liked his outdoor hay and leather scent.

She wasn't clueless. She knew she was attracted to him.

He was also her employer, a fact he'd made loud and clear.

Still, for now, she was content on the Sundown. After a few weeks, she'd begun to relax. Her body grew stronger, healthier. The nightmares came less frequently.

Most evenings, after the triplets were in bed, she'd walk through the hay meadows and fields until sundown, away from distractions to pray and absorb the calming effect of the surrounding Kiamichi.

Usually she'd spot a cardinal or two, and her thoughts turned to the nearness of God, the beauty of His creation.

Sunsets on Sundown Ranch took her breath away. Never had she felt so close to God as she did when she watched the sun drop behind the mountain, and the first shadowy veil of evening spread over the land.

Sometimes she lived through an entire day without remembering the tornado. A true gift.

"Hey." The quiet male murmur broke her thoughts and turned her face toward the doorway.

Her heart jittered. She continued to rock the child in her arms.

A sock-footed Wade, his brown hair mussed from his hat, eased into the nursery. He held a bouquet of Indian paintbrush in one hand.

"Truce?" he whispered, solemn and contrite.

Those rascally jitters got worse.

A smile lifted Kyra's lips. She nodded.

Rising, careful not to disturb the baby, she took Ben to his crib and eased him onto the cool sheet. When Benjamin raised his sweaty head and stared at her, she froze, waiting. Then, apparently satisfied, he flipped his face to the other side and lay down again. The teething pain must have subsided for now.

Thank You, Lord.

Wade moved silently to the crib and gazed down at his son. The heat and scent of the outdoors radiated off his body. His arm and right side connected with hers.

He looked from his son to her, his eyes holding hers for a long moment before he glanced down again.

Though the connection was innocent, it felt intimate, as if they were a couple.

She was acutely aware of his muscled arms, of *him*, of the tenderness flowing in the nursery. Maybe it was caused by her peaceful thoughts. Maybe it was Wade himself.

Maybe it was both of them and these little babies.

For a nanosecond, she imagined that this man and the triplets belonged to her. That she was more than the temporary nanny.

A mood floated through her. A yearning. She longed to put her hand on Wade's where it gripped the top rail of the baby bed. His attention remained on Ben, but she saw the movement of his throat as he swallowed. Was he feeling this, too?

Suddenly, he turned away from the crib and left the room.

Giving the sleeping triplets one final glance, Kyra followed.

Obviously, he'd not felt what she had.

But Wade had offered a truce. She was a peacemaker who disliked conflict.

The flowers were thoughtful, too.

She found him in the kitchen, pouring tea into a glass. When she entered, he tipped his head toward the pitcher. "Want some?"

"Sure." She got her own glass, filled it with ice from the front of the fridge and let him pour the tea for her. "What happened to our truce?"

"Still on." The wildflowers lay on the counter. He handed them to her. "I was mad at Keno this afternoon, not you."

Kyra lifted a shoulder. "You're my employer." Which was true, regardless of the strange, alluring mood in the nursery.

"You had every right to expect me to be with the triplets instead of standing on the back porch while you and that sumo wrestler in a cowboy hat argued."

His mouth quivered. "Sumo wrestler?"

Chuckling, she rolled her left shoulder and rubbed the stiffness in her arm where Ben had been sleeping.

Wade's gaze snapped to the spot. "Something wrong with your arm?"

"A little stiff from rocking Ben."

"How long?"

"An hour. Maybe more. His fifteen-month molar is trying to come through, and he couldn't get comfortable anywhere else."

"He's taken to you. All of them have."

She wanted to ask if he had, but that would be a dumb move.

Sundown Ranch was a respite, a summer job, a way of easing back into the workforce with children. She had not come here to fall in love, certainly not with a man who still carried uncertain but volatile feelings for the mother of his triplets.

"I love them, Wade. Each of those babies is a unique and special little human being."

"You looked real good with him in your arms that way. It looked right."

Meaning what? That he was pleased with the job she was doing? Or something more?

And why was she reading so much into a simple compliment?

"What's the deal with Keno?" she asked to hush the voice in her head. "I couldn't hear all of the conversation, but he does not seem to be a nice man."

"That's an understatement." Wade took his tea to the bar, tossed a leg over a stool and gestured toward the opposite seat. "He's suing us, though our lawyer says he doesn't have a leg to stand on."

"That's good, isn't it?"

"Being in the right is good, but fighting him to prove it won't be cheap. Lawyers cost money. A lot of it."

She tickled the back of his hand with the Indian paintbrush. "Maybe you should take him some wildflowers."

He smiled at her joke. "If only flowers would do the trick. Peace offerings, which, believe me, I've tried, have no affect on Bud Keno or his boys. Kenos have hated Trudeaus for generations, and the current father and Bill, the eldest son, have taken the feud to new heights. The younger two are showing signs of feeling the same. No one in my family remembers why they hate us. Kenos probably don't, either, but they keep the feud going."

"I heard you and Bowie discussing a cut fence. Did a Keno do that?"

He nodded. "And that's not all. Untagged calves disappear, gates are mysteriously opened and more. Mischief mostly. Then they blame us if our bulls get in their pasture."

"I don't understand people like that. People who'd rather have trouble than peace." She circled the tea glass on the granite countertop. "My dad would say they can't stand to see others happy because they have a big empty spot inside where God should live."

"Your dad is a wise man."

"He'd also tell us to pray for them and for an opportunity to speak God's light to them." She flashed her eyes to his, not wanting to sound too preachy. "I'm sure you've done that."

"Maybe not enough. Talking to the Kenos in a peaceful manner isn't easy, especially now. The situation wasn't this bad until Yates left."

"Yates?"

"Yeah." He rubbed a hand over the back of his neck, expression pensive. "My prodigal brother. He and Keno had some kind of understanding. Keno was a little afraid of Yates, I guess." He spread his hands. "Or something."

A prodigal brother?

"Tell me about Yates." She was prying, but he seemed willing to talk, and she wanted to know him better. She didn't, however, want to consider the reasons.

"Not much to tell. Yates is my oldest brother. He left a long time ago and refuses to answer my calls or come home."

"Did something happen between the two of you?" When his face darkened, she put a hand on his sun-browned forearm. The muscles had gone tense. "I'm sorry. None of my business."

"No. It's okay. Not something I usually talk about." He took a long swig of tea and observed the condensation drizzling down the glass.

"We had a younger brother, Trent. He was fourteen. Yates and I were young adults. So was Bowie. His mother brought him to live with us when we were little, so Bowie's more of a brother than a cousin. Anyway, when my folks were killed in a plane crash, Yates, Bowie and I were pretty young, but old enough to take over the ranch and look after Trent."

"I'm sorry, Wade. I didn't know about your mother and dad." So very sorry. She knew how sudden tragedies could change a person's entire life. "I can't imagine losing my parents. And in such a tragic manner."

He wagged his head, one finger tracing a single drop down the glass. "Wasn't easy. That's for sure. I still miss them. Always will."

"Is that why Yates wanted to leave? The shock?" The way she'd had to get away from Tulsa?

"Not at first. He loved this ranch. He's the best working cowboy you'll ever meet. But then Trent died…"

His voice trailed off. He clamped down on his jaw, his mouth a hard line. His knuckles whitened against the tea glass.

More death. More heartache. He'd lost more, had seen more tragedy than any person should have to handle.

Yet, he'd soldiered on, even though it was clear his heartaches hadn't ended with his brother's death.

Her admiration for him elevated another few notches.

"Don't break the glass," she said softly as she lightly tapped his clenched grip.

Evidently, Trent and Yates presented a problem he didn't like to think about.

What could be worse than losing his parents and brother?

One by one, Wade noticeably relaxed his fingers.

When he didn't go on with the story, Kyra said, "We don't have to talk about this."

He gulped another long drink of tea and set the glass on the counter with a hard thud.

"Trent's death," he said at last, "was my fault. I killed my brother."

Kyra kept her gaze and voice steady. She understood guilt. He was a frequent companion of hers.

"I don't believe that. Whatever happened to your brother must have been an accident."

"Accident or not, I caused it. He's dead because of my negligence."

"Guilt is a hard thing to live with, Wade." Didn't she still hear Tristan's voice in her dreams, and sometimes when she was awake? "Have you talked with anyone about your feelings?"

"You mean like a counselor or a pastor?" He shook his head. "Pastor Blake offered, but what's the point? Trent is dead. Talking won't change a thing."

"Getting your feelings out in the open, though, might change you." She smiled, a little embarrassed. She was a preacher's kid. Offering advice and a listening ear was in her DNA. "I'm sounding like my dad. I'd apologize, except he's a great counselor."

He put a hand over hers and squeezed. "You are, too."

After two beats when he didn't move his hand, she let herself enjoy the contact. The pesky tingles started up.

"Will you tell me what happened?"

"Are you sure you want to hear it?"

"I do."

He pondered her face for a long moment as if he expected her to shy away. When she didn't, he took in a long breath, blew it out and began.

"I was supposed to be with him. With Trent. Yates had told me to go, but I had a hot date." He made a wry face. "Nineteen and crushing on a girl whose name I don't even remember now. You know how it goes. So I sent Trent to the bull pasture by himself."

Nothing about that sounded ominous. "Had he gone alone before?"

"A few times, but Yates was a worrier and preferred us to work in pairs around the bulls." Wade's voice grew small. "From what we later surmised, one of the young bulls went on a rampage and crushed Trent against his ATV. It was the worst thing I've ever seen in my life."

He closed his eyes as if reliving the horrific scene, his expression wreathed in grief.

A knot formed in Kyra's throat, hard and tight. "Oh, Wade, I'm sorry. That's horrible. But it wasn't your fault."

"Yates thought it was. Me, too. If I'd been there, Trent would still be alive."

"You can't be sure of any such thing. Being present isn't always enough." She'd been with Tristan, only a few feet away, but she'd been as helpless as he was. "Some things in this life—and everything in death—are out of our control."

She'd struggled with that hard truth for a long time. Still did. Though her rational mind knew better, some part of her thought she should have been able to save Tristan's life.

She understood Wade's feelings far better than he could imagine.

"People make choices, Kyra. My dad used to tell us boys that all the time. God presents choices. It's up to us to make the right one. I didn't that day, and my selfish decision cost my little brother his life."

"You'll have to forgive me if I don't agree. The ultimate decision in life and death belongs to God."

He made a huffing sound. "I've wrestled with that, too."

So had she.

"Why Trent? Why not me? Why, after losing our parents, did my brother die, too? He was such a good kid." He tilted his head back, his chest rising and falling in a heavy sigh. "Man, I loved that boy. We all did. He was the baby, the favorite. You would've loved him."

The ache in his words tore at her tender heart. "What was he like?" Sometimes talking about the loved one soothed the wound of loss. Another of her dad-isms she'd found to be true.

"Athletic. Goofy in a fun kind of way." A tiny twitch of cheer creased the skin around Wade's eyes. "He always had this big cheesy grin on his face and you couldn't make him mad even if you tried."

Kyra nodded, feeling the mood lighten as he recalled the good things. "I never had a brother, but I know kids. You probably tried."

"Oh, sure. He was the baby, so Bowie and I tormented him, all in good fun, of course. Short-sheeted his bed, hid his boots, sent love notes to girls signed with his name. Trent never took offense. He'd laugh and laugh, and then he'd pay us back." Wade shook his head, finally allowing a nostalgic grin. "Don't even ask me about the plastic wrap across my toilet lid."

A giggle tickled its way up Kyra's throat. She pressed her fingers to her lips. "Sorry, but that's funny. You're right. He sounds like a great kid."

"He was. Yates, being the oldest, would sometimes tell Bowie and me to back off, leave the kid alone. So naturally, Trent thought Yates hung the moon."

"What about you?"

"Yeah. Me, too. Yates was the big brother everyone should have. Protective, smart, a strong leader." He pulled a hand down his face, effectively wiping away the pleasant nostalgia of moments before. "If he'd only come home…"

His voice trailed off, his thoughts lost in the brother who'd left him with a load of guilt and sorrow and loneliness.

"When did he leave?"

"Right after Trent's funeral. Packed up and left. No goodbyes. Just gone. Both of my brothers gone in a matter of days."

He turned her hand over and laced his fingers through hers. "Sorry for dumping this on you. You're a good listener. Maybe too good."

"Pastor's kid. I've also had a few counseling sessions from Dad over the years." Hours and hours since the tornado.

"Well, thanks. I hope you don't think less of your old boss now that I've spilled my guts all over you."

"No reason to. I loved hearing about Trent and Yates." She smiled, though the action held more sad tenderness toward the rancher than joy. "Thank you for trusting me enough to tell me."

"Yeah, well…" With a self-conscious chuckle, he untwined his fingers from hers. "Guess I should get back to work and let you do the same."

He pushed off the bar stool, reached for his hat, which lay upside down on the kitchen counter, and was gone before Kyra could wrap her head around his sudden departure.

Chapter Eight

That night, after he and Kyra had put the triplets down for the night, Wade worked on the books for a while before hitting the shower.

He considered a trip to the bunkhouse to talk to Kyra some more.

Caution won out.

This afternoon, he'd felt closer to her than he had to anyone in a long time. He'd been mildly surprised to look down and discover he'd twisted his fingers with hers.

For those brief moments with Kyra in the kitchen, he'd remembered how much he enjoyed the differences between a woman and a man. Even the way she listened and encouraged was feminine. Sabrina had pounded all the good things about women out of his memory bank.

The feel of Kyra's smooth skin against his calluses lingered still, a reminder of what had been lost, drowned and swept away, in a sea of heartache and anger.

Bowie could be right. He might be attracted to Kyra. As in romantically attracted. Kiss face and all that feel-good but potentially trouble-causing business.

Considering the triplets' need for a nanny, he'd keep those crazy thoughts to himself.

When Kyra had thanked him for trusting her, he'd been shocked, bothered, shaken. He didn't trust her. He didn't trust any woman, no matter how attracted he might be.

His eyebrows tugged together.

Talking wasn't trusting. Was it?

Stretching out on his oversized king bed, Wade stacked his hands behind his head and watched the ceiling fan move lazily above him. Like his emotions, the fan went in circles and never got anywhere.

One thing for sure, trust or not, talking with Kyra about Yates and Trent had gotten his brain cells whirling. About his big brother, especially, and the close bond they'd once shared. About the discontent in Yates after Mom and Dad had passed. About how much Wade missed his brother and wished he could see him again. Most of all, he wished for Yates's forgiveness.

If he knew where Yates was, he'd jump in his truck and drive there right this minute, tonight, no matter how far he had to go.

What kind of family was so broken that a brother refused to come home or call or even reveal his location? Eight years, eight lousy years since he'd last seen his only living brother.

Wade's heart ached so much he could feel the squeeze beneath his rib cage.

Closing his eyes against the pain, he prayed for his prodigal brother.

The last time they'd spoken, Yates was running to catch a plane, deployed to military duty in some secret destination. No doubt a hot spot or danger zone. Wade didn't know exactly what his brother did for the military, but Yates was never one to shirk the most dangerous or grueling task.

Probably why Bud Keno had steered clear. Yates had a temper and could clean a man's plow at the drop of a hat. He could be tough and resolute where Wade tended toward mediation.

Since that last deployment more than three years prior, Wade had received a few terse replies to his texts but no answered calls. Since the triplets' birth, he'd heard nothing at all. Not even a congratulatory text.

Wade reached for his cell phone and scrolled through until he found the old photos he'd transferred to his phone. The four Trudeau boys, Wade, Yates, Bowie and Trent, hamming it up, unaware that life would soon tear them apart.

Nostalgia as thick as lemon pie and every bit as bittersweet settled in his bedroom like an old acquaintance.

Finding Yates's number in his contacts, he shot a text.

Call me.

Then, when he'd hopefully snagged his brother's attention, he pressed the call icon, praying that this time Yates would answer.

The *brrr* vibrated against his eardrum over and over until finally clicking into a generic voice mail message.

Disappointment moved in. It was always like this. He'd call, leave a message and Yates wouldn't respond.

When the beep sounded, he whispered, "Miss you, brother. I'm sorry."

Sighing, he pushed End and let the cell phone fall against his chest.

Kyra closed her devotional and put it aside.

Had she heard something?

She leaned forward in the easy chair to listen.

Living in the country was so different than the city.

Contrary to popular opinion—mostly from city dwellers like her—the country wasn't silent. It was calming, less hurried, but there were plenty of noises.

Were those footsteps she heard?

The hair rose on the back of her neck. She reached for her cell phone. Here in the cabin, she could receive decent service, thanks to a booster Wade had installed.

A light tapping sound came, as if someone hesitated to knock.

Eyebrows coming together, her thoughts went from fear to worry.

Had something happened to one of the triplets? Did Benjamin need her?

She leaped from the chair and hurried to the door. "Who is it?"

"Wade."

She opened the door a tiny crack.

Wade, looking freshly showered in a white T-shirt and faded jeans, his hair slightly damp and curling at the crown, lifted a bag of microwave popcorn and a DVD. "I couldn't sleep. I saw your light."

Kyra's heart executed a somersault worthy of the Olympics. He'd seen her light and come calling? Why?

"What about the babies? Who's watching them?" Undoing the security chain, she let him in.

"Asleep. Bowie's on duty."

"Everything's all right, then? How's Benjamin?" *And why are you here if nothing is wrong?*

He put a hand on her shoulder.

"They're great, Kyra. Stop fretting. Ben barely wiggled after you rocked him and put him down."

Some of her tension eased away. "Oh, good. Maybe the worst is over."

"For him. Not for us." With a wry twist of his lips, Wade lifted three fingers and then lowered one. "One down, two to go."

"Poor babies." She offered a one-shouldered shrug. "Such is life with three toddlers."

"Tell me about it. I had no idea how hard it would be to care for three kids at once."

"Me, either."

"Seriously? I couldn't tell. You have a natural, easy way with them."

He wouldn't say such nice things if he knew how anxious she was at times, worrying that something would happen to one of them or that she'd fail them the way she'd failed Tristan.

"That's because you help and in desperate moments, so does Bowie." She didn't know how else she would have managed.

"Desperate moments? You mean like when you're changing one baby and you hear the toilet flush, and the other two babies have disappeared, toting stuffed animals, which can wreak havoc on your plumbing?"

"Ah, the voice of experience." She chuckled. "And I'm not trying to run a ranch at the same time. A full-time nanny with help is much easier than one dad and three babies."

"Are you saying we make a good team?"

"I think we do." The ramifications of that statement were not lost on her.

And she was reading *way* too much into a simple conversational statement. They were a team, friends, employer and employee. That was all.

Looking a tad uncertain, Wade remained standing inside the bunkhouse door as if he might dash away at any second. He'd been inside before, mostly to help her carry something, but not in a while and never late at night.

Why had he crossed the driveway tonight?

Was this afternoon's conversation still weighing on his mind?

A current passed between them, the sizzle of attraction she felt every time they were together. He felt it, too. She could tell by his sharp intake of breath and the way his bewildered gaze settled on hers.

This sizzle thing was, indeed, bewildering.

"You can come into my *living room*." Kyra put the words in jaunty air quotes, determined to keep the mood light and friendly. "I've moved it closer to the kitchenette." She pumped her eyebrows. "Where the snacks are."

Wade pointed a finger at her. "Smart woman."

His boots made thudding noises, softened by the giant area rug she'd place in the center, as he followed her to a cozy corner with two easy chairs, a TV and a small coffee table.

"I like what you've done." He made a wry face. "But considering the alternative…"

Remembering, her lips curved. "We've come a long way since that first dust-covered day."

"Yes." His eyes smiled into hers. "I think we have. A very long way."

What exactly did he mean by that? Was she, once again, reading more into the statement than he'd intended?

Again, she wondered why he'd come knocking this late. Not that she wanted him to leave. She didn't.

Perhaps that was the issue.

"I doubt you came over tonight to compliment my decorating skills."

The uncertainty in his expression returned.

"If I'm bothering you. Or keeping you up too late—" he stabbed a thumb over one shoulder "—I can hightail it back to the house."

"No, no. Not at all. I wasn't sleepy yet." Truth was her

energy had shot to double-espresso level the moment he'd walked in the door. She didn't know why he was here, but she was glad he'd stepped over the barriers he seemed determined to keep between them and crossed the driveway. "Was there something you wanted to talk about?"

That couldn't wait until morning?

A terrible thought hit her. Wade wasn't about to fire her, was he, because of their earlier disagreement? Not after he'd declared a truce and they'd had such a deep conversation.

Yet, after their heart-to-heart, he'd hurried out of the house as if he wished he'd said nothing at all.

While these worrisome thoughts flashed through her mind, Wade handed her a DVD. "I figured after our bar stool counseling session, I owe you a movie and popcorn. A thank-you or an apology, whichever it requires. What do you say? You, me and Denzel Washington?"

Relief rushed in, and she thought how silly she was. Wade needed her. The triplets needed her. He wasn't about to fire her. He was grateful, and unless her radar was completely messed up, Wade Trudeau liked her company. She liked his, too.

Flipping the DVD over, she glanced at the movie title. "This looks good, and I appreciate the gesture, but I don't have a DVD player."

Shoot. Now he'd leave. And she didn't want him to. The two of them rarely had time alone.

Wade opened his mouth, closed it, opened it again, stacked his hands on his hips and looked defeated. "So much for my great idea."

Exchanging looks, they both grinned. If their gazes held an extra beat or two, she wasn't complaining. A man with those kind of eyes was meant to be looked at.

"All is not lost," she said with more hope in her tone

than she'd intended. "There's probably something amazingly bad on TV. Or if our timing's good, we might find a classic."

Kyra caught herself and stopped. She was behaving as if this were a date, and Wade had come over with the expressed intention to be in her company. He'd brought the movie as a thank-you, nothing more.

He hoisted the microwave bag. "Somebody's gotta eat this popcorn."

A smile lit her insides. "Absolutely."

With a satisfied grin, he tossed the DVD on the coffee table, picked up the remote and started channel surfing while she stuck the popcorn in the microwave.

In minutes, they'd settled in their respective chairs, a bowl of buttery-scented popcorn serving as a buffer between them while they watched a corny old melodrama that was more funny than sad.

At one particularly maudlin part, Kyra faked a sniffle. Wade pretended to gag and then bopped her in the side of the head with a popcorn fluff.

"What?" She squinted at him in mock anger. "Aren't you finding this Oscar-worthy?"

"I'm pretty sure my IQ has fallen ten points in the last ten minutes."

"A point per minute. Whew! At that rate, you'll run out of brains by the movie's end. And then what?"

He hit her with another shot of popcorn.

"Hey!" She grabbed a handful and peppered him, one fluffy projectile at a time in rapid-fire sequence. Her softball skills, which she'd eschewed as worthless, were coming in handy.

Wade dipped and ducked, returning fire and laughing in a way she rarely heard from the overworked, harried cowboy daddy. Popcorn flew around the room, bouncing off the TV, the walls, each other.

Kyra laughed so hard, her throws lacked much velocity. When one shot fell a good two feet short, Wade pointed, smirking, his blue eyes sparkling with humor. "That all you got, noodle arm?"

"I'll have you know I was an ace second baseman. *Ace!*" She gave the next throw her all, beaning him between the shoulder blades as he twisted his anvil-shaped torso to one side.

Wade needed this. So did she. *A time to laugh*, like the Bible said. A time to play and forget their worries.

This playful Wade seemed more approachable, more real and, if such a thing were possible, more appealing.

When they'd emptied the bowl and popcorn lay strewn about the space, they fell back against their respective chairs, faces turned to grin at each other.

Kyra's pulse raced from the exertion. Her breath puffed, short and quick. So did Wade's.

Except for the television neither of them wanted to watch, the only sound was their breathing.

After a bit, she said, "That was fun."

"Yep. Movie's going off," he said. Though he never turned his head to look at the TV, his mouth twitched. "Thank goodness."

"No kidding. How's the IQ?"

Using the heel of his hand, Wade bopped the side of his head a couple of whacks. "Shaky as ever."

Kyra emitted a tired laugh.

"Want me to make more popcorn? I have some in the cabinet."

"Nah. There's plenty on the floor if I get hungry enough."

Kyra snorted.

Until now, she hadn't realized what a fun sense of humor Wade had. Which only made her like him more.

Another movie began, but neither of them paid it any mind. They began to talk, at first about the triplets and the ranch, steering clear of the afternoon's painful discussion of Wade's brothers.

The conversation veered into other topics. Movies they actually liked or wanted to see. Favorite music. College. He was an Oklahoma State Cowboy, naturally. She graduated from Oral Roberts University.

After they'd good-naturedly argued about which was best, they moved on to their faith, their favorite scriptures and when they'd come to know Jesus. He asked her opinion of the Sundown Valley Bible study she'd begun attending, and they discussed the topics and the friends she'd made there.

He seemed especially interested in her opinion of Becky, Shawna and the other women she'd met. When she admitted to enjoying their company enough to make a lunch date, he seemed oddly relieved.

When he asked about her work as a teacher, Kyra stumbled over her reply. Although she considered telling him about the devastating tornado, she didn't. Wade had enough tragedy in his life. He didn't need to carry her burden, as well.

"You miss teaching," he said after she'd waxed nostalgic about some of her students.

"I do, but my hands are full right now with the triplets." Her heart, too.

"You'll go back in September." His expression had grown solemn.

"Probably. Hopefully." She was healing. She could feel it. Other than an occasional bad dream, she'd not had one flashback episode. Her mind and spirit were more rested, more at peace, quieter these days. God was preparing her for a return to her former life in the classroom.

Wade stared at the flickering TV, silent, pensive.

"You'll find another nanny by September," she said, confident that his sudden withdrawal was concern for the triplets.

"Yeah." He didn't sound convinced, and for good reason, she supposed.

The older woman who'd cared for the triplets since birth was the only person who'd ever applied for the job. Miss Janey had only agreed because she'd been friends with Wade's late parents and attended the same church. The kind woman had felt sorry for a man whose wife had abandoned him and their infants.

Replacing her as nanny might not be easy.

"It's late." Wade stood, found a piece of popcorn in his chair and tossed it at her. "I should go."

"I'm glad you came over. This was fun."

"It was. Thanks." Yet, some of the energy had seeped out of him. Tired, probably.

She followed him to the door where they both paused.

"I have a doctor's appointment in Tulsa next Friday," she said. "Would you mind trading days with me, and I'll work the weekend in exchange?"

Alarm flashed in his expression. "Are you sick? Is something wrong?"

She held out a hand. "It's only a checkup."

"Sure. Take the day. Whatever you need." He rubbed a hand over the back of his neck and stretched his head from side to side as if the muscles had tensed. "Why don't we trade Friday for Sunday. That gives you two full days with your family. Then come back on Saturday night and attend church with us on Sunday. If you want to. No pressure."

Warmth spread through her. "I'd love to."

"Good. It takes an army to get the triplets ready and out the door on Sunday morning."

Right. The triplets. He'd invited her to church because of them, not because he wanted her company.

And he was right. She'd taken the dynamic trio into Sundown Valley to shop a few times. Traveling with three babies took the logistics ability of a field general.

She admired Wade for running the baby gauntlet every Sunday. A lesser man would have used the triplets as an excuse to skip church.

His faith was real and deep, like hers.

Reaching around her, Wade opened the door and stepped out on the wooden porch. Clean green-scented night air, cooler than the June day, enveloped them.

"Look at that." His voice was hushed.

"What?" She stepped out with him.

To the right, the night spread over the land, dark as ink. To the left, pale yellow security lights illuminated the main house and nearby barns.

He pointed toward the darkness. Tiny points of light flickered above the grass near a line of woods.

"Fireflies?"

"Lightning bugs, my brothers and I called them, but fireflies is a cooler term."

Delight filled her. She clasped her hands together. "We don't see them much in the city."

"No, I guess you wouldn't." He slid the flat of his hands into his back jeans' pockets.

"Too much light, I'm sorry to say. Even the stars and moon are brighter here on the ranch, in the country. The sheer nearness of nature makes me feel closer to God. All of this, the stars, the mountains, the woods, is his design, his handiwork."

"Do I hear a poem stirring?"

Wade turned his head to smile down at her, and then

looked back toward the fireflies and the inky diamond-laden night sky.

"Maybe." She'd told him about the poems she'd begun writing again since moving into the bunkhouse. His kind reaction encouraged her.

The moon had risen, a cantaloupe slice cradling a bright twinkling star.

"When I look at the night sky," she said, "and see the work of His hands, the moon and stars He set into place, what are mere humans that He should even consider us at all, much less that He should care for us?" She tilted her chin toward Wade's profile. "I didn't write that. It's too beautiful."

"Psalms?" The deep timber of his voice carried a smile.

Pleased, she nodded. "The Kyra paraphrase. Dad used to quote it every night when we camped in these woods and mountains. He taught us to see God in everything."

"Nowhere is He more visible than in nature and the ranching life." Wade pivoted slightly, angling his body closer to hers. So close that she whiffed his shower soap. "Ranchers live close to the land. My parents taught us not only to use the land as a livelihood, but to love it, respect it, care for it, and to remember that God ultimately controls everything. He's given us stewardship, but we're only borrowing it for a while."

"He's blessed you here on the Sundown."

"Yeah," Wade murmured as if he hadn't considered his blessings in a while. "Yes, I guess He has."

Not wanting him to leave or to disturb the peaceful aura that had settled over them, Kyra asked, "What's that pulsing noise? Frogs?"

"Tree frogs. Crickets. Katydids. They all have rhythmic mating songs. Summer sounds."

"They don't sing in the winter?" She'd never been to

the mountains in winter. What would it be like here in chilly December or frigid January?

"Winter is real quiet out here," Wade said. "Coyotes mostly."

Shivering a little at the thought of coyotes or wolves, she moved a half step closer.

He looked down at her, his face serious. "Scared?"

"No." She rubbed her upper arms. "Not really. I just don't want to be a meal for predators that howl in the dark."

He smiled.

"I won't let them get you." The gentle teasing timbre of his manly voice caused tingles on her skin.

"My knight in cowboy boots?" Her tone dropped low, hushed and tender.

In the dim shadows of the porch, Wade turned to face her. The tree frogs' song seemed to throb in Kyra's chest.

For a long, pulsating moment, she thought he might kiss her.

And she wasn't sure what she'd do if he did.

Her heart yearned toward him. But they were employee and employer, and she had a job to do here.

Yet, she could not deny that sizzle of attraction.

"Kyra," he started.

She tilted her head in question.

His fingertips grazed her cheeks. A delicious shiver raced down Kyra's spine. She liked his hands, the strength, the hard work she could feel in them.

When she started to lean into his touch, his hands fell away.

"Good night."

Then he stepped off the porch and faded into the darkness.

Chapter Nine

Wade fumed as he, Bowie and Riley wrestled a pile of rocks and logs blocking the creek.

A half-dozen cows and calves meandered the bank, bawling and jostling for a drink of the normally spring-fed stream.

"No doubt who did this." Riley kicked at a log in frustration, his face dark with fury.

"Keno knows this section of the creek is the only water source for this particular pasture." Wade wiped a shirtsleeve across his sweating face. "If you hadn't been checking fence, these cows could have been in trouble fast."

"Yeah. And *he's* suing *us*. How does that make sense?" The usually mild-mannered Bowie glared at the obviously man-made dam holding back the water. The stream, with its origin in the mountains, was the purest, freshest water on the Sundown Ranch.

"It doesn't make sense. Not a lick. But like always, the Kenos are sneaky and we can't prove they did this." Wade had snapped photos of the dam to share with their lawyer, but he didn't expect them to make a difference in the lawsuit.

True to his threat, Keno was moving forward with the frivolous legal action.

Wade kicked a rock, an action he instantly regretted. The dull pain shot through his boot leather like a stubbed toe.

Today, his frustration was about more than Keno trouble.

Last night, he'd almost kissed the nanny.

She'd probably have slapped his face.

No. She wouldn't have.

There lay the trouble.

He liked her a lot, and he was pretty sure she liked him back.

"Riley," he said, more to get his mind off Kyra than anything, "you'd better ride the other fences. Most likely this is the only trouble area, but with the Kenos you never know."

"I could take the east fence," Bowie said.

"Weren't you going into town for more baling twine?"

"Yes, but—"

"—I got the fence. No problem." Riley removed a bandanna from his hip pocket and wiped sweat from his mustachioed face before mounting his horse and riding away.

After Riley's departure, Bowie said, "He likes riding fence."

"So do you."

"Yeah. Peaceful."

"Except for when it isn't." Wade wiped sweat again and glanced at the sky. "The humidity today is killing me."

"Might storm later."

"Maybe. Remind me to clean the storm shelter out."

Bowie waved him off. "I already did it. The babies and all. Didn't want to chance it with the new nanny."

Just like that, Kyra was back in Wade's head.

Before his brain could engage, his alligator mouth blurted, "I almost kissed her last night."

With a grunt, Bowie tossed a heavy rock onto the bank and then turned a mild gaze on his cousin.

"Told you."

"Don't be stupid. It was a mistake. I realized it at the last minute. I mean, it was dark outside and we were watching lightning bugs and stars and standing kind of close. The next thing I know this urge to kiss her rose up like a tidal wave."

"Watching lightning bugs? And stars? Together. Uh-huh. Kind of romantic."

"It wasn't supposed to be. I went over to thank her and next thing I know we're having a great time together. She's so easy to talk to, and she's pretty and sweet. And she's wonderful with the triplets."

"You're falling for her."

"I can't." Frustration building, he heaved the biggest rock he could find. He'd probably have a backache tomorrow.

Sometimes Kyra's back bothered her. He'd noticed how she pressed her hands to her lower vertebrae. She took ibuprofen nearly every day. He'd seen her do it. Were the triplets too heavy for her?

He heaved another rock, this one lighter.

"I hear you," Bowie said. "Too much like Sabrina."

She was. Except she wasn't.

During last night's conversation, she'd admitted how eager she was to leave the Sundown and head home to Tulsa as soon as her time here was up.

You can take the woman out of the city, he thought, but she'll go back. This was a vacation of sorts, a respite. Even though, when he'd hired her, she'd claimed to need a break from teaching, last night she'd revealed the truth. She was eager to return to the classroom.

But, his brain argued, she loved the mountains. Her family enjoyed nature, loved camping.

Most likely her dad had one of those fancy RVs that was more like a hotel than true camping. Somehow, he couldn't see a Tulsa girl roughing it in a tent.

There was a lot about the nanny he didn't know.

But he wanted to know everything.

Irritated with the direction of his thoughts, he insisted, "She's the nanny. She's here to care for the babies. That's all."

Bowie grunted. "Whatever you say."

"She won't be here on Friday. I'll have to take off work to watch the triplets."

"Scared her off last night, did you?"

Wade scowled his opinion of that statement. He hoped he hadn't scared her away.

"She has a doctor's appointment in Tulsa."

Bowie paused in their seemingly endless efforts to clear the stopped-up creek. "Is she sick?"

"That's what I asked her. She says no. Only a checkup. But her back bothers her a lot. She doesn't complain, but I noticed."

"You sure notice a lot about a woman who's only the nanny." His cousin gave him another of those mild looks that spoke volumes.

Wade was tempted to toss a rock at him.

The way he and Kyra had tossed popcorn at each other. Silly, but fun. When had he simply let himself go and had fun like that?

Not since Sabrina came into his life. No, even before that. Life had stopped being fun when Yates had disappeared.

Maybe Bowie was right.

He noticed everything about Kyra. The shine in her red hair, the changeable color of her hazel eyes, the way she smelled too good. Mostly, he noticed the way she mothered his babies.

Mothered.

Something Sabrina had never done.

Remembering his ex-wife's selfishness made his heart

hurt. Her treatment of his babies made him angry, too, and solidified his reasons for not getting involved with another woman. Women could eviscerate a man and destroy the security of their children.

He wouldn't chance anyone hurting his kids again.

Kyra was an employee, not a relative. She got paid to care about his children. For three short months.

He'd best remember that, too.

On Friday morning, after her doctor's appointment, Kyra stopped by the pastor's office at the church where she'd grown up.

When she walked in, her dad pushed away the stack of correspondence he'd been reading and got straight to the point. "What did the doctor say?"

"They ran another MRI." She made a face. Lying in the tube with the top pressing in toward her face wasn't her favorite activity. Not being able to move reminded her too much of the hours beneath the tornado rubble. But she'd gotten through without a panic attack, something she hadn't managed in the early days of the injury. "Dr. Jacobson only saw the preliminary report, but he thought everything looked good. Great, even."

"Glad to hear it." His smile lit up his eyes. Eyes the same nondescript hazel color as hers, though his hair was fair where hers was red like her grandmother's. "How goes the nanny job?"

A picture rose in her head of Wade, his face in shadows, his fingers touching her cheek.

She felt a hint of a blush heating her neck. "The triplets are wonderful, Dad. Benjamin finally cut his molar, but now I think Caden's is trying to come through. And Abby is starting to say actual words. Yesterday, Wade walked into the house and she yelled, 'Dad!' It was so cute."

Those hazel eyes contemplated her face for a long moment as Dad leaned his elbows on his desk and clasped his hands together. "You're enjoying them."

"Yes, of course. You know how I feel about kids."

"But these are special. I hear it in your voice every time we talk."

Though they texted often, their real conversations came in person on weekends.

"They're precious, innocent babies who need all the love anyone can give them. They're adorable and funny and energetic and exhausting." She laughed. "Watching them explore the world is a gift. Yesterday, Benjamin shared his pancake with me, and that boy does not like to share."

Her insides warmed at the sweet, sticky memory.

"Are you getting too attached, honey, considering your plan to teach again in the fall?"

"It's hard not to, Dad. I worry how Wade will manage once I leave. He's trying to find another nanny, but Sundown Valley is a small town."

"So you're getting along well with the children's father, too? You feel safe there?"

"Very safe." She didn't mention the problems with the Kenos. "You should drive down sometime and meet Wade and spend the day with me. He's a good Christian man, Dad, a hard worker with a good head on his shoulders. He's wonderful with his babies, and I'm told he was very active with his church's youth before the triplets were born. I think you'll like him."

Her dad's gaze rested on her again, discerning. "Sounds like you are also getting attached to the babies' dad."

Kyra and her parents had always been close, but during her recovery, the relationship between her and her dad had deepened. Sharing her concerns with him was second nature.

"I'm not sure. Maybe. Probably. I like him a lot. And when we're together…" She shrugged, embarrassed not to be able to put her feelings into words.

"Your heart beats a little faster and you feel lighter and happier?"

"Yes." Might as well admit it.

"Does he feel the same?"

"I don't know that, either. Sometimes I think he does. Not that there's been anything romantic going on between us." Not really. The night on her porch had been an aberration, a moment out of time. They'd been tired, and emotions run amok when people are tired.

"Tread lightly and be wise. I'm your old dad, and I'm still concerned about you even though you're a grown woman."

"I'm cautious, Dad, especially after Sean." Smiling, she pointed a finger at him. "But remember what you taught me about worry."

"Practice what I preach, huh? Take my concerns to the Lord in prayer." His smile was amused.

"Exactly. And while you're praying for me—" she stopped to give him a knowing look "—if you would, please pray for Wade. He's had a lot of heartache in his life."

She told him about Trent and the estrangement from Wade's older brother. She kept Wade's overreaction to any mention of his ex-wife to herself. But she prayed about his anguish just the same.

The phone on her father's desk jangled. He held up one hand. "Excuse me a minute."

Accustomed to these interruptions, especially when they were in the church office, Kyra sat back and pretended not to listen.

Of course, she heard every word.

When he hung up the phone, her father looked a bit

uncomfortable. "That was Lisa. I've asked her to join me for dinner on Sunday."

"Lisa Coleman?" Something in her father's expression warned her. "Are you and Lisa dating?"

Though she'd never thought about it, her dad was an attractive man and still plenty young enough to find love again.

When Mom was alive, Dad had fiercely guarded against being alone with a female parishioner, though several had been obvious in their pursuit of the handsome, eloquent pastor.

But the idea of him with a woman other than her mother stunned her.

"Would you mind?"

Did she?

And even if she did, what right did she have to deny her father a chance at finding love again?

"Of course not."

During the long year of her recovery, Dad had been at her side. Other than his pastoral duties, he'd had no social life. She'd never considered how lonely he must have been.

"Lisa is a lovely woman. A devoted Christian. And if she makes you happy, then I'm happy for you." Shocked and unsettled, perhaps, but truly glad for the man who'd sacrificed a great deal for his daughter.

Getting used to the idea of seeing him with another woman, though, would take some doing. And a lot of prayer.

Sunday morning, Wade walked into the white-framed church in Sundown Valley with Kyra at his side. They were early, as he tried to be, considering how long it took to get the triplets settled in the nursery.

Heads turned, and he could practically hear the wheels

turning in nosy heads. His friends knew Kyra was the nanny. They knew she attended their age group's weekly Bible study. The other congregants, however, didn't know, and speculative glances rippled through the church.

Small towns loved to talk, and he and Kyra had given them new meat to chew on.

The Sundown Valley grapevine stretched all the way to the ranch. Now it would bear lots and lots of fruit.

Once the babies were in the nursery, he took Kyra's elbow and guided her to his usual spot four rows back from the altar. Regardless of gossip, Wade felt proud to have her at his side. She was beautiful. And she smelled great. Like sunshine and flowers.

He filled his lungs with her perfume as he shook hands and introduced her to those nearby.

The fortysomething pastor, Blake Cloud, came out of his study and stopped for a chat. "Kyra, it's a pleasure to see you again. How are you enjoying Bible study?"

"I love it. We've been discussing the book of Ephesians and I'd forgotten how rich and deep it is." She laughed. "I call my dad after every session to discuss it with him."

"How's your dad doing?"

"He's well. Thank you for asking."

They exchanged a few more pleasantries before someone called Blake's name and he turned away.

Kyra's eyes followed the Native American reverend. "He seems like a great pastor."

"He's been there for me, for all of us, anytime we've needed him." Through the loss of Trent and the abandonment of his brother and wife, Blake visited, texted, called and prayed with him so many times God surely felt sorry for them both. "Our church is thankful to have him."

The piano began to play, a reminder that service was about to begin. North Cross was a traditional church, different, Wade knew, from the more contemporary nonde-nominational services Kyra was accustomed to.

He handed her a songbook. She looked down at it and then back at him as if she'd never seen a hymnal in her life.

A sudden clutch grabbed Wade's throat.

Would Kyra appreciate the small-town church? Or turn up her nose at the old-fashioned hymns and traditionally structured service?

"What did you think?" Wade asked as they exited the church following the benediction.

Leading one toddler while Wade and Bowie each held hands with another, Kyra walked toward the pickup truck. "I loved it. 'Great is thy Faithfulness' is one of my favorite old hymns, and as soon as the singing started, I felt peace flood over me."

A late June sun already threatened to heat up the world, and she was glad for the cool, peach and cream dress she'd worn with beige sandals. The tea-length hem swirled around her calves, stirring the breeze.

"Good." Wade sounded relieved as if he'd expected her to criticize. "I'm glad."

Abby tugged her daddy to a halt and reached for a pebble on the pavement. Wade hoisted her into his arms. "Pastor Blake can get pretty wound up. I didn't want him to scare you off."

Kyra smiled in an effort to ease Wade's anxious expression. "My dad's style may be different, but anyone who preaches biblical truth is fine with me. The sermon was excellent. Hard to hear in places, but good for us. For me, anyway."

"I needed to hear it, too. For sure, we can't pick and choose which parts of the Bible we like and leave out the hard parts."

"As Dad would say, truth isn't always easy to hear, but it's the key to resisting those temptations that might sound good at first, but that harm us in the long run." With a chuckle, Kyra shook her head. "Sorry. I always seem to be quoting my dad."

"Nothing to apologize for. He sounds like a great dad and pastor. He sure raised a fine daughter."

Kyra flashed a glance his way. Today he'd worn a turquoise dress shirt that made it impossible not to stare at his eyes. "I invited him to drive down for a visit sometime. If he does, I'd like for you to meet him."

The skin around those vibrant eyes crinkled. "I'd like that, too."

His reaction pleased her. Though their lifestyles differed, Kyra was confident Wade and Dad would hit it off.

A friendly relationship between the two men was starting to matter to her.

When they reached the truck, she and Wade took turns strapping the triplets into the rear baby seats. Once the babies were settled with a toy, and the back doors were secured, Wade turned to her and Bowie, who had tagged along to help with the babies.

"I'm starved and not in the mood to cook. Let's grab Sunday dinner at Dave's." To Kyra, he said, "Have you eaten at Dave's? It's a great family-friendly restaurant. Really good fried chicken and pot roast."

"I haven't, but eating out sounds terrific. I don't want to cook, either."

"Then it's decided. How about you, Bowie? You coming?"

"No." Without further explanation, the cousin looked at Wade, gave a small laugh and headed to his truck.

Kyra frowned after him.

What was that all about?

* * *

Dave's Restaurant was noisy with cheerful-sounding conversations and after-church diners. Families in their Sunday best and others in casual clothes gathered at square tables or in padded purple booths. The friendly atmosphere smelled wonderful—like yeasty hot rolls dripping in butter.

Guided by two servers carrying high chairs, they wound their way toward an open table.

Not surprisingly, the triplets drew lots of attention. During the meal, other diners, some who knew Wade and others who were simply attracted by a set of three dark-haired babies, paused at the table to chat.

She was glad she and Wade had dressed the tots for church with extra care so they looked as cute as pie. The boys wore matching knee-length khaki shorts with yellow golf shirts and sturdy walking shoes. Abby matched them in a sunny yellow dress and headband bow with the cutest little white sandals and lacy socks.

The trio were definitely attention grabbers, and Kyra's heart swelled every time someone stopped to exclaim about their adorableness. As if they were her babies. As if she had a right to receive the compliments.

Eventually, the visitors disbursed and the food was served.

"This looks amazing." She sniffed the steaming pot roast with mashed potatoes and brown gravy. "And the smell!"

Wade had ordered the same. With a pleased smile, he said, "They cook from scratch, the old-fashioned way."

"For which I am thankful."

"Speaking of thankful, let's pray." He bowed his head and murmured a short blessing.

Ben yelled in disgust at the delay in his dinner.

Wade put a hand on the child's arm and said, "Amen."

Abby grabbed for the hot rolls, but Kyra was too fast for her. "One at time, little miss cuteness."

She tore off a small portion and handed it to Abby and was rewarded with a bright, "Tank oo."

Kyra and Wade traded proud looks that held.

The family feeling that was never far away rose inside Kyra, tall and strong and flexing an ever-thickening muscle.

Warmth spread up her neck and over her cheeks when Wade continued to stare, the softest smile barely tipping his lips.

The attraction was like a cord stretching across the table, tethering their hearts together.

And she was being ridiculous.

Except her heart didn't think so.

To break the spell, Kyra blinked and turned away to offer Caden a green bean.

"No." Caden's head swung back and forth as he rocked away from Kyra's outstretched hand.

Both adults stared at the baby. Wade spoke first. "Did he say no?"

"He did." Excitement rose in her voice. She grabbed Wade's hands and squeezed. "Wade, that's his first word!"

Wade laughed, his pleasure real. "Leave it to my kid. Instead of Da-da, his first word is *no*."

With a fondly knowing gaze at Ben, Kyra said, "He probably learned it from his brother."

Wade's laughter deepened. Oh, how she loved his laugh. "Or from Abby. She likes that word, too. Especially at bedtime."

Aware that she still held his hands prisoner, Kyra released him and sat back in her chair. "So true."

She offered the rejected green bean to Ben, and he

crammed it into his mouth, then stuck out his tongue and let the offending vegetable fall to his high-chair tray.

"Green beans are not garnering any fans today."

A server stopped to top off tea glasses and bring applesauce for the triplets. The pureed fruit was a hit with all three babies, although a messy hit.

Kyra whipped out a pack of wipes from the diaper bag and began cleaning faces as a well-dressed couple stopped at the table.

"Wade, I thought that was you. Your little ones are precious." The perfectly coifed woman wiggled Abby's reaching hand.

Kyra grimaced. Abby's hand was loaded with applesauce.

When the woman pulled back and looked at her soiled fingers, Kyra grimaced and offered her a wipe. "I'm sorry. Right now, they're a mess."

"Babies are messy, and dealing with so many of them at once. My goodness. I can't imagine."

The woman's words weren't intentionally snarky, but they raised Kyra's hackles just the same.

She didn't *deal* with the triplets. She loved them. Yes, they were a challenge at times. Yes, they were lots of exhausting work. But they were pure joy packed into three small bodies. This strange woman had no right to demean them.

Wade held a hand toward Kyra, and she slapped several wipes into his wide palm.

He must have felt her tension because he said, "Kyra Mason, meet Ted and Liz Cohen. Ted's my attorney."

His wife nudged the attorney's arm. "But you didn't stop to talk business, did you, Ted?"

"No, no. We can do that tomorrow. I'll give you a call." The lawyer reached inside his suit jacket. "Liz is committee chair for the July Fourth Independence Day celebration." He handed Wade several tickets. "We thought you and your girlfriend would enjoy taking the little ones to the carnival and petting zoo."

Kyra looked up from wiping Caden's chin. Again. "But, I'm not—"

Wade interrupted. "That's real nice of you, Liz. Thanks."

The couple said their goodbyes and moved on, but Kyra couldn't get their comment out of her thoughts. She wasn't a giddy teenager. Naturally, people assumed a man and a woman were a couple if they were dining together, especially when children were involved.

But her silly heart had leaped like a kangaroo at the mere mention of being labeled as Wade's girlfriend.

And he had not disabused them of the notion.

Wade tapped the tickets against the table edge. "What do you think?"

"They seem very nice."

"No. I mean, about Independence Day. Would you like to go with me? It's a big event for Sundown Valley. Carnival, rodeo, ball games, three-legged races, picnic, fireworks, you name it. Maybe take the triplets to the petting zoo?"

She'd love to. She'd love sharing the babies' delight. And she'd love being with Wade, though he was only asking her because the couple had brought up the topic. And because he'd need help with the triplets.

But should she? Should she allow herself to get any more involved on a personal level when she would be leaving at the end of summer?

What difference did leaving make? Tulsa wasn't that far away.

Too far, however, for a real relationship. Which they did not have.

Who was she kidding? Wade had been clear from the

start. He still harbored deep feelings for his former wife. Kyra would be crazy to let herself fall in love with a man who pushed her away at every turn.

"I'm scheduled to be off work on the Fourth, remember?" If she stayed in town to attend the celebration, she'd be working, not on a date. It was best if she reminded herself, and him, of that fact.

"Oh. Yeah. I forgot." With slow deliberation, and what looked for all the world like disappointment, he slid the tickets into his shirt pocket and glanced at his watch. "Nearly nap time."

"For you or the babies?"

"Both." He smiled at her joke, but it was a sad smile that left her troubled.

As they gathered the triplets to leave, Kyra wondered. Had Wade invited her as a date and not as a nanny? Was he disappointed?

She certainly was. Which was totally senseless, considering the mental counseling session she'd given herself.

Hoisting a triplet into each of his strong arms, Wade led the way to the door. As he used his body to open and hold it as she passed through with the diaper bag and Abby, he said, "I could have won you a teddy bear at the carnival."

Her pulse, that untamable rhythm, did a Snoopy dance.

Chapter Ten

The triplets climbed and swung and raced around the small playground in Sundown Valley's municipal park, cackling and squealing with the pure joy of life.

"They're having such a good time, Shelby. Thank you for inviting us on this playdate."

"I'm glad you agreed. This gives you and me a chance to hang out and get better acquainted. We have so little time to visit at Bible study." Shelby, a short bubbly brunette, was married to one of the town's police officers and seemed to know everyone in Sundown Valley. "Besides, Austin loves playing with other kids, and being an only, he needs the socialization."

Shelby had been candid about her fertility issues. Austin was likely to be her only biological child.

An old worry niggled at the back of Kyra's brain. After she'd been crushed in the tornado, the docs warned that she might not be able to bear children. Since those early days, the subject hadn't come up again, but she still thought about it now and then.

First, though, she needed a husband.

Wade's handsome face flashed behind her eyes. Yes, she was falling for him. Falling hard.

A sniffling Caden toddled toward her, holding out a tiny palm covered in grass. He'd taken a tumble and appeared near tears.

"You're okay, baby sweetness." Kyra wiped away the

grass and smacked a kiss right in the center of his little hand. "See? All fixed up."

The sad expression disappeared. Caden gurgled out a reply and hurried back to his pals.

"These babies adore you."

"I adore them in return."

The bag crinkled as Shelby withdrew a potato chip. "How are you and Wade getting along?"

"Fine."

Shelby, sitting beside her at the concrete picnic table, gave her an elbow nudge. "I mean, how are you *really* getting along? He's a good guy. Hard worker. Runs a successful ranching operation. He's no slouch in the looks department, either."

"Can't argue that."

"So, what gives?"

"I'm the nanny. He's my boss."

"Oh, brother." Shelby crunched another chip in disgust. "Seriously? I saw the two of you at church. You're so cute together, and you're telling me there are no sparks?"

"Sparks are overrated."

Shelby hooted. "Now you're talking."

Kyra held out a hand, stop-sign style. "There is nothing romantic between us, Shelby. For real. Wade's still hung up on his ex-wife."

Shelby rolled her green, green eyes. "That woman, don't get me started. Sabrina Myers is a piece of work. And yes, she went by Myers, even after they married. She's beautiful, but as shallow as a dry pond." She hitched both shoulders up close to her ears. "If I sound judgy, I am only judging her by the fruit she bore, and that's perfectly scriptural."

Kyra chuckled.

"Well, it is," Shelby said with a sniff. "Sabrina was a drama queen, self-centered and spoiled. She treated all of us in Sundown Valley like we were ticks on her favorite poodle."

Very descriptive. And sad. The citizens of Sundown Valley were, for the most part, good salt-of-the-earth people. "But Wade loved her. He married her."

"Men are blind sometimes, especially when a woman is as beautiful as Sabrina. We're talking high maintenance, movie-star gorgeous, tons of lush brown hair, huge violet eyes and long shapely legs up to the moon."

Which made Kyra feel as attractive as a dishrag. She wasn't even close to beautiful. Presentably pretty, but not gorgeous.

"She wasn't from this area?"

"Definitely not. I'm not sure where they met, but she was not a small-town country girl."

As Kyra pondered this bit of information, the wind picked up and sailed a napkin from the table. Kyra trotted after it. Ben considered this a game and toddled to help. She scooped him up for a kiss, letting him carry the napkin back to the table.

Shelby was frowning at the sky. "Teddy warned me that we might be in for a storm today. I should probably head home. He frets unless Austin and I are safe and sound if the siren blows."

"Siren?"

"Tornado warning. Don't worry, it only blows if a tornado is spotted in the area."

As if someone had poured ice water down her back, Kyra shivered. Not a storm. *Please, dear Jesus, not a storm.*

While they'd talked and the kids had played, thick dark clouds had rolled in. The sun had disappeared. The air felt hot and sticky.

Panic rose in her throat. She swallowed it. There was nothing to get upset over.

There hadn't been a tornado in Oklahoma in over a year. And she hadn't had a flashback in months. She was fine. The babies were fine.

Wade had a storm shelter.

She needed to get them home.

Quickly, she stuffed the remains of the picnic lunch into a bag, deposited trash in the nearby containers and called to Abby, Caden and Ben.

"You can come to our house until this blows over if you want," Shelby offered.

"We're okay. I'll head to the ranch."

A gust of wind whipped her hair back from her face.

"Call me when you get there."

"Will do." When another gust of wind pushed Abby onto her bottom, Kyra grabbed her and Caden and ran toward Wade's truck, put them inside and hurried back for Ben who was fighting the wind to keep up.

Fat droplets of rain struck the windshield as they drove away from the park.

"It's only rain," she said, more to herself than to the babies buckled into the back seat.

The wipers flapped a rhythm against the windshield, smearing dust and rain.

"It's only rain," she said again. "God is watering the flowers. We are safe."

Plenty of rain had fallen in the last year. She could handle rain.

But her heart pounded and her mouth had gone dry as baby powder from the moment Shelly mentioned the word *tornado.*

A jagged bolt of lightning split the sky in front of the car. She jumped. A tiny shriek slid between her lips.

Don't scare the babies. Take care of your charges. They are your responsibility.

Thunder rumbled, deep and loud. More lightning

flashed. The dark clouds lit up, flickering like fireflies, only far more terrifying.

Help me, teacher.

Her chest hurt. Unwanted images of that terrible day pressed in. Flashing, like the lightning, until she wasn't sure where she was.

Clinging to reality, Kyra fought against the flashback.

"The babies. I have three babies. I have to get them home. Remain focused." She clenched her teeth together hard, struggling to remain in the present.

What would happen if she lost control? If she forgot where she was? Something terrible could happen to Wade's children. She must protect the children.

Teacher. Teacher!

Hands gripping the steering wheel, she prayed, "When I am afraid, I will put my trust in You. I trust You, Lord. I trust You. You are my strength and refuge, an ever-present help in time of trouble."

Rain pounded Wade's truck as she guided it the ten miles from town to the ranch, murmuring every scripture that rolled through her mind.

By God's grace and mercy, she made the drive in one piece.

As she turned into the driveway, her fingers trembled so badly she couldn't work the garage remote.

Suddenly, the door rose as if by mental telepathy.

Wade stood inside the structure, waiting.

She'd never been so thrilled to see anyone in her life.

"Thank you, Jesus." She pulled in, turned off the key and leaned her forehead on the steering wheel. They were safe. The babies were safe.

Wade opened the driver's-side door. "Are you okay?"

She lifted her face. "Is there a tornado? The babies. The babies. Hurry."

She must sound like a madwoman.

He put a reassuring hand on her arm. "No tornado, Kyra. Only a thunderstorm. A fierce one, but we'll weather it."

Tears sprang to Kyra's eyes. She batted them away. "Oh. Thank God."

"Hey, now. You're all right. Everything's all right."

He reached for her, and she fell into his arms, shaking so hard she thought she might fall to the concrete floor and dissolve into a hysterical puddle.

As if Wade sensed her fear, he pulled her shivering body close to his very warm, sturdy, chest. Solid. Safe. Caring.

"Storms scare you?" he whispered against her hair.

She nodded, unable yet to explain the reasons.

Wade stroked her back, murmuring reassurances, as tenderly as he did for the triplets.

She'd been afraid, and he'd instinctively embraced her.

But the touch of his lips against her ear was a different matter.

A reaction, surely. Nothing to ponder.

More importantly, she hadn't lost control. She'd fought off the flashback. She'd brought the triplets safely home.

Everything *was* all right.

Slowly, her heart rate settled and the shaking ceased, though she felt as weak as a newborn kitten.

After a bit, the storm inside abated. Kyra sucked in a long breath and on the exhale said, "We should get the babies inside. They must be scared."

"They're asleep." His quiet baritone rumbled above the rain pounding outside the garage.

"Asleep?" Reluctant to be out of Wade's strong, comforting arms, she turned only her head toward the back seat. Three sets of eyes were closed in peaceful rest. The triplets had slept while she panicked.

There was a lesson there somewhere. She'd think about it later.

She rested her cheek against Wade's chest, aware of his steady, confident heartbeat, and sighed in contentment.

She'd needed him, and he'd been here for her. No questions asked, no mockery. He'd simply pulled her into his arms and made her feel safe.

"I thought," she whispered, when the dryness freed her tongue, "I was going to have a flashback. I was afraid of losing control and letting something happen to the triplets."

He eased her back a little to look into her face. "Flashback?"

"PTSD. I should have told you before you hired me, but I thought I was over the worst of it. I would never have intentionally endangered your children."

"PTSD?" His eyebrows slammed together. "From what? What happened, Kyra?"

The concern in his tone made her brave. She should have told him before. Now she did.

"A tornado warning came over the school intercom, but I couldn't move fast enough. Several of my students were in wheelchairs, others had limited ability to fully comprehend the danger. I got most of the children out with a paraprofessional, but then the tornado struck, loud and powerful. The whole world turned upside down. Boards and bricks and desks flew around us. The ceiling crashed in and—"

Kyra stopped. Her heart hammered wildly, as if the organ would escape her rib cage and fly away. Her throat had thickened, shutting off her air.

Now was not the time to flashback to that awful day.

Sensing her distress, Wade began the soothing back rubs again. "I've got you. You're okay. Safe and sound right here in the garage with me. I've got you."

Bless him. He'd instinctively reoriented her to the garage, understanding the danger of PTSD.

Kyra nodded, swallowing the thickness, taking a deep shaky breath.

"Tristan. He was eight. A second-grader." She bit her lip, fought the grief. "I heard him calling me. *Teacher, teacher!* I could see him. But I couldn't reach him. Oh, Wade, I tried so hard."

Her words broke on a sob. She reined it in. Gulped. Started again.

"I dug and scratched." She looked down at her hands, curled against broad shoulders. "I didn't even notice my bloody fingers. They didn't matter. I had to save my kids. But I couldn't. I couldn't."

Tears leaked from her eyes. She hid her face against Wade's shirt, though this time she didn't fight off the emotion. Tristan was worth her tears.

"You tried, honey." Wade's deep voice choked with emotion. He snugged her closer, his heart as tumultuous as hers. "I know you tried."

"He was trapped upside down in his wheelchair, his face only inches from a floor rapidly filling with water." She closed her eyes against the memory, but it was there, waiting, like always. Haunting and guilt inducing. "A ton of debris and bricks covered me from the waist down. I could only move my arms."

She shuddered in a breath, leaking it out in a painful whisper. "After a while…he didn't call out anymore."

The memory of that terrible silence, broken only by the shifting bricks and the distant sirens, was forever etched on her soul.

She'd broken three fingers fighting to dig free in those last awful, silent moments before it was too late to save him. And she'd failed.

"He drowned. My sweet little Tristan with the biggest smile you've ever seen died because I couldn't reach him."

Wade tipped her chin upward with his strong fingers, blue eyes filled with compassion, sharing her grief.

"I'm sorry. So sorry. But I know you, Kyra. If it had been in your power to save that child, you would have. You were hurt, too."

His thumbs stroked her face, catching the tears she couldn't seem to stop.

"My back was broken in a couple of places. A few other injuries, too."

Wade shook his head, as if in disbelief.

"My strong, amazing Kyra." He kissed her then, a kiss of compassion, of comfort, as gentle as the ones he gave the triplets. A tender touch of lips.

Her foolish heart reacted as if they were a great romance for the ages.

When the too-short kiss ended, he studied her tear-stained face for several seconds before, embarrassed, she forced herself to pull away. "I'm okay now."

"You sure?" His long rancher's hands rested on her shoulders. Strong, dependable hands that could wrangle a bull or soothe a baby. Or a panicked woman.

"Yes. Thank you for…being kind." *For holding me. For kissing me.*

"Kind," he whispered as if to himself. "Yes. Kind."

A beat passed while the rain drilled the roof and Kyra longed to step back into his arms.

She didn't, though.

If she'd been confused about her feelings—and his—before, she was even more bewildered now.

The Sundown Valley Independence Day celebration was in full swing. And Wade wondered why he'd come at all.

Being a divorced dad instead of married or single was no fun. He felt old and lonely, pushing a trio of tots around in a triple stroller all by himself.

Bowie was here somewhere, probably silently grinning at a girl or two who were trying to coerce him onto the Ferris wheel. He might ride the Ferris wheel or even go on a date, but the relationship would end there. Bowie never let anyone get too close.

Wade had watched him go through the cycle a dozen times. Bowie was a nice guy, a great friend, the man to call in a time of need, but his heart was as closed off as a top security military base.

He had a good notion why his cousin was so wary, but they never talked about Bowie's parents or the scars he carried deep inside. Maybe that was the problem with the Trudeau boys. They held too much inside, and it ate away at them like rust on an old '57 Chevy.

Pausing at the cotton-candy stand, Wade ordered a cone of the fluffy sugar. The girl who waited on him smiled at the triplets but barely noticed their dad.

Such was his life now.

He shoved a wad of spun sugar in his mouth. Normally, he'd find some friends and tag along. Today, he felt all out of whack and wouldn't be good company for anyone.

He and Bowie had come to the festivities in different trucks, so Wade was on his own with the triplets. As it should be. Bowie was single. He should be mingling with the ladies and his pals.

Later, there'd be a rodeo. Bowie and Riley wouldn't miss that. In the pre-dad days, Wade wouldn't have, either.

Not that he'd trade one hair on his babies' heads for all the rodeos in the world.

Still, he'd be lying if he said he didn't miss the old days on occasion.

In spite of the heat, the triplets were doing great. They'd

watched their first parade from the shaded sidewalk, alternately clapping and staring, although Caden and Abby had cried when a clown came too close. They'd squealed with glee at the high school marching band, though.

After the parade, he'd pushed their stroller around the fairgrounds for a while, visited old friends, stopping at the petting zoo where he'd snapped photos to share with Kyra.

He missed her. So did the babies. Abby had asked more than once for Kee, her name for Kyra.

Since the thunderstorm episode in the garage, he'd tried to be more circumspect with the nanny, more thoughtful.

The story she'd shared had shaken him, twisted his guts. He'd give anything if he could erase the trauma from her life. Kyra was strong, though. She'd survived and thrived.

One of the things that kept playing in his head since that thunderstorm was the way she'd focused on the triplets. She'd fought off a panic attack to protect his three babies, to get them safely home to him. Her concern had been for them, not herself.

The same way she'd fought to save her students.

The story of her bloody fingers, her broken body, the awful tragedy had nearly done him in.

He'd wanted to absorb her grief and carry it for her.

Then he'd gone and done something crazy. He'd kissed her. And he'd wanted to go on kissing her for days and days.

He'd meant the kiss only as comfort, but it had become much more. He'd felt the impact clear to the toes of his Justin Ropers. But a man like him, a bitter country cowboy who'd been dumped by a city girl, had no business locking lips with another one. Not again. Not when he had three children to protect.

Kyra had protected them, too.

Wade shoved another wad of pink fluff into his mouth.

He couldn't deny his growing feelings for Kyra. But they'd laid out the ground rules from the beginning. Three months. He wouldn't risk his heart and those of his triplets. They'd had enough loss in their short lives.

He paused to rescue a dropped sippy cup and adjust the canopy over Abby. She babbled at him, Ben played with a whirly red, white and blue pinwheel, and Caden shouted, "Dad-dad-dad."

His chest expanded with love. They melted him, these three nuggets, and no matter how alone he felt at times, he thanked God for them.

A calliope pumped music from the area of the carnival, a small affair set up a distance from the bounce house, sack races and food vendors. From here, he spotted the Ferris wheel and heard shouts and laughter as feet dangled from rocking seats high above the crowd. He saw no sign of his cousin.

The luscious smells of the barbecue cook-off drifted through the air. His taste buds hummed.

The sun slid toward the western horizon, taking some of the heat with it.

He thought about skipping tonight's fireworks, grabbing a plate of barbecue, calling it a day and heading for the house. The loud firecracker noises would probably scare the babies, anyway.

Suddenly, a pair of cool hands covered his eyes from behind. Female hands. His heart jumped. Had Kyra changed her mind and returned to Sundown Valley?

"Guess who?" a voice said against his ear.

A voice that wasn't Kyra's.

Gently, he reached up and removed the hands, turning toward the speaker. Jessica Wallace, a woman who'd once shown considerable interest, stood before him in short shorts and a patriotic tank top smiling a little too brightly.

Apparently, her interest had returned.

He wished he could say the same.

"You all by yourself?" she asked.

"No." He lifted his eyebrows pointedly toward the stroller.

"Oh, silly, you know what I meant." She flapped a hand at him and giggled. "Are you here with someone other than your kids? A girl, maybe?"

His thoughts, those disobedient things, went straight to Kyra. "No."

"Great. Let's hang out."

He wasn't up for it. Not with Jessica, anyway. But instead of refusing, he tossed the ball in her court. "I could use some help taking the triplets on the carousel."

Jessica shrugged. "Sure. Okay. But didn't you know one of the churches has a childcare service going on? A local youth group is raising money for missions or some such thing."

"That's my church."

Her expression brightened. "Great. Let's drop off your kids and go have some real fun."

Wade bristled.

"My kids *are* fun, Jessica." Kyra thought so. "They're my life now."

Saying it out loud made him feel better. To prove the point, he led the way to the carousel. After the ride, Jessica made excuses and disappeared into the crowd.

He couldn't say he was sorry. He didn't mind leaving the babies for a few hours now and then, but any woman who considered his triplets a burden to be dumped somewhere wasn't a woman he wanted in his life.

Not like Kyra, who loved his kids and enjoyed every second with them.

Or at least, he thought she did.

Maybe it was an act. Maybe she was all about the fat check he gave her every two weeks.

Growing disgruntled, he started toward the truck. Home was the best place for him today.

Taking the most direct route through the carnival midway, he passed the workers hawking darts or balls for a chance to win a prize. Light bulbs dangled over the booths, lighting the ever-darkening way.

The sun would set soon. Kyra loved sunsets.

Suddenly, familiar laughter hit his ears. He stopped the stroller to stare through the milling crowd.

Was that Kyra?

Of course it was. He'd recognize that red hair anywhere. Today, she wore a ponytail that swung when she laughed.

And she was laughing up into the face of a man. Jay Fleming. The real-estate agent.

What was she doing with him?

They stood at the counter of a dart game. Jay hurled darts like a madman while Kyra laughed and clapped her hands.

Why hadn't she called or texted if she was returning to Sundown Valley today?

Or had she been planning to attend the festivities all along with Jay? And hadn't wanted to share that bit of news with Wade. Had Kyra intentionally misled him?

Scowling, Wade pushed through the crowd, a knot in his belly and his jaw clenched.

The awful insecurity left by Sabrina swept in, a tidal wave. He had no right to feel angry or jealous or whatever this hideous feeling was that was ripping his insides.

Kyra didn't belong to him. They weren't a couple. She could date whomever she chose.

But he'd thought she cared about him enough to be honest. He desperately needed honesty after Sabrina's betrayal.

As he pushed the babies closer to the dart game, fighting emotional turmoil, Kyra turned slightly and spotted them. A bright smile broke over her face.

"Kee, Kee, Kee!" Abby bounced up and down in her seat. The boys reacted, too, with wildly gyrating arms and indecipherable language.

Wade slowed. Face alight, Kyra didn't look the least bit guilty.

She put a hand on Jay's arm and said something. Jay handed her a pink fuzzy boa and then waved toward Wade.

Wade's nod was short. The knot in his belly had moved to his throat. His chest hurt, too, as if a horse had kicked him in the sternum.

Draping the boa over her shoulders, Kyra said something else to Jay and then strode toward Wade.

He glared at her, wondering.

When she drew near, her smile faltered. A tiny frown pulled between her golden eyebrows. "I've been looking for you."

Sure she had. That was why she'd been laughing with another man, a man who'd won her a prize at the carnival.

"You could have texted."

"I wanted to surprise you."

"You succeeded." He turned the stroller and began walking toward the parking lot.

Kyra hustled to catch up. "Are you upset about something?"

"Why would I be?"

"I don't know. That's why I'm asking. Because I'm getting really strong vibes from you that you're angry at me about something."

"Why were you with Jay if you were looking for us?" There. As childish as he sounded, he'd spoken his thoughts.

She grabbed his arm and stopped his fast retreat. "We ran into each other at the dart game. I was trying to win a prize and failing miserably."

"So he offered to win one for you."

"That's right. He did." She wiggled the boa against his arm. The feathers tickled. "Now I am the proud owner of this lovely fake boa that's making my neck sweat."

At her jaunty, innocent teasing, some of Wade's steam seeped out.

Feeling suddenly stupid and childish, Wade paused beneath a shade tree and stacked his hands on his hips. "I thought you'd lied to me."

Her head drew back. "About?"

"You said you were celebrating in Tulsa with friends and family."

She bent to kiss Ben's extended hand, declaring him delicious and yummy. The baby grabbed for the boa and slid it from her shoulders. She let him have it.

"I changed my mind."

He wondered why. But didn't ask. His insides still roiled.

He shouldn't be upset. He had no right, except maybe he wanted to have that right. Which scared him out of his mind.

After the number Sabrina had done on him, he didn't know if he'd ever trust another woman. He wanted to, but held out little hope of that ever happening, especially when a small incident like this one shot holes in his self-esteem and turned him into a suspicious jerk.

Another reason to ignore his growing feelings for the nanny.

If he couldn't trust himself, he sure couldn't trust someone else.

Chapter Eleven

The Fourth of July didn't go exactly the way Kyra had planned. Wade was in a terrible mood, for reasons she couldn't understand, and had left soon after she'd found him at the carnival.

He'd used the triplets as an excuse to go home to the ranch, but she strongly suspected his attitude had something to do with her.

Was he angry because she'd come back earlier than planned?

But that didn't make sense. Why would he care? She hadn't interrupted anything or interfered with him in any way.

So what was the deal?

After a cookout with friends and family in Tulsa, she'd decided to drive back to Sundown Valley for tonight's fireworks show. If she were honest, she'd hoped to watch them with Wade.

He clearly had other plans.

Like what? To sit at the ranch and stare at the TV while the triplets played or slept?

That didn't make sense, either.

With a sigh, she gave up worrying about Wade for now to look around the fairgrounds. She'd never attended a small-town function like this and decided to stroll the grounds and soak up the atmosphere. Even for someone alone, the event was fun, festive and safe.

Families with their children filled the place. Which

made her think of Wade and the triplets again. If he'd stayed, they could have been enjoying a family outing together.

She shook her head in disgust. He and his kids were a family. She was the nanny. She had become way, way too attached to the Trudeau family.

Even if she toyed with the idea of being more than an employee, Wade sent up so many mixed signals she got a headache trying to sort them out.

As the sky darkened, the smell of smoked meat tempted her taste buds. She bought a barbecue sandwich and iced tea at a concession run by a local service club and sat down at one of the many awning-covered picnic tables found throughout the fairgrounds.

Attending a festival alone felt odd, but she saw people she knew, mostly from church, but some from businesses around town.

She bit into the spicy-sweet sandwich and watched two teenage boys try to impress their girlfriends at the strong-man game. Jockeying like peacocks, they took turns slamming a hammer onto a lever as they tried to ring a bell at the top of a tower.

"What are you smiling at?"

At the male voice, Kyra looked up to find Bowie at her table.

She hitched her chin toward the game. "Those boys. They're trying so hard to impress their girlfriends."

"A man thing." He looped a leg over the opposite bench and joined her. "I thought you were in Tulsa."

She was surprised some woman hadn't latched on to the quiet, gorgeous cowboy. "Was. My cookout and swim party was this afternoon, so I decided to come home for the fireworks."

Home. Was she really considering Sundown Valley as her home?

"Does Wade know you're here?"

"Yes." A hot wind stirred the air, and Kyra brushed a few stray wisps of hair from her face. "He wasn't in a great mood so he took the triplets home."

Bowie's shoulder jerked. "His loss. Want to watch the fireworks show? I'm meeting other friends, but you're welcome to join us."

"I'd like that. Thanks."

She finished her sandwich and, taking her cup of iced tea, walked with Bowie. They didn't talk much at first. She'd grown accustomed to his long silences.

Eventually, he asked, "What ruffled Wade's feathers?"

She tried to explain, although she wasn't sure herself. "He thought I lied to him."

The tall Cajun gave her one of his long thoughtful looks. "Sometimes my cousin is an idiot."

After that cryptic statement, they were swallowed up by a group of friends and Kyra had no further chance to ask exactly what Bowie had meant.

"You're an idiot."

Wade clicked off the TV and stared at his cousin. The mildly spoken sentence lingered in the living room like the smell of burned beans.

It was late. Bowie had just returned from the night's festivities. He'd walked into the house and, without preliminaries, had declared Wade an idiot.

He was probably right.

Unable to sleep, Wade had watched some of the fireworks from the backyard after the babies were in bed. With the ranch on a rise above the valley, the display was visible above the trees.

They'd reminded him of the night he and Kyra had looked at the stars together. And he'd started missing her all over again.

"Did you hear me?" Bowie planted his booted feet in front of Wade's recliner.

"Loud and clear."

"I sat with Kyra at the fireworks show."

He hadn't expected that. Wasn't sure he liked it, but who was he to object? "So?"

"You should have been there. She wanted you to be."

In another life, he would have been. But this was the life he had to lead. "Can't risk it."

Bowie tossed his hat onto the couch and sat down beside it. "Coward."

Wade took offense at that. He was a lot of things, but he was not, never had been, a coward. "I have three kids to consider."

His cousin sighed, long and loud and tired-sounding. "She's not Sabrina."

"No, she's the nanny. And she'll be leaving in less than two months."

"Look. I get that you're bitter. If anyone understands, it's me. I was there, remember? But sometimes a man has to close the door on the past and walk through the one that's opened right in front of him."

Bowie understood about leaving the past behind. His own life had been trampled by the very people who were supposed to care about him the most. Yet, somehow, he'd picked up the pieces at the tender age of ten and kept moving.

Not that he'd had much choice.

"Was Kyra okay?"

"Ask her yourself." Hands to his knees, Bowie pushed up from the couch and left Wade to stew in his own juice.

Such was his cousin. He didn't say a lot, but when he did, Wade knew to listen.

He picked up the remote. Tossed it down again.

After a few minutes, he went to the window that looked out toward the bunkhouse.

Her lights were still on.

Without letting himself think too much, he shoved his feet into his boots and exited the house.

The July night was sticky hot, but beautiful with a clear starry sky. In the distance, fireworks still boomed now and again, silencing the insect songs. Probably kids down on the lake, the place he and his brothers had gone as teens to show off and pop fireworks.

He stepped up on the bunkhouse porch.

What would he say to her? That he was a bitter man who'd never again trust a woman enough to have a relationship?

Maybe. Or maybe they'd just talk. He liked talking to Kyra.

She wouldn't get the wrong idea.

They were friends.

Yes, friends.

The little imp in his brain, which sounded a lot like Bowie, laughed.

Kyra had seen Wade's shadowy figure as he'd crossed the driveway beneath the security light. And she'd heard his boots thud against the wooden porch. But he hadn't yet knocked.

She waited another twenty seconds and then opened the door. "Are you going to stand on my porch all night like a Peeping Tom?"

"May I come in?"

"Sure." She pushed the door open farther and let him pass. "Want something to drink? A Coke maybe? It's hot tonight."

"Sounds good."

She fixed them both a soft drink while he settled at her tiny two-person table.

As she joined him, he said, "I'm sorry about today. I was a jerk."

"Yes, you were. And I still don't understand why."

"Me, either. Not really." He shook his head. "That's not true. But my lousy mood had nothing to do with you." He cleared his throat, took a swig of soda. "It's my ex-wife."

Kyra gulped the drink she'd taken, almost choking on it. This was the first time he'd mentioned his ex-wife without fury.

An unexpected frisson of unease skittered up her back. "Was she there? Did you hear from her?"

He scoffed. "No. Never."

"Not even to inquire about her babies?" She could hardly believe any woman would be that callous.

Wade's chin shot up. Blue eyes arced fire. "They're *my* babies, not hers. She signed over all rights. All they have is a daddy. Not a very good one, either."

"That's not true, Wade. You're a great dad. Being both mother and father is a task not many could handle, especially with three. But you do it."

The corner of his mouth curved. "You didn't always think that way."

"That was before we were friends. I know better now." Regardless of his long work hours, Wade found time to stop by the house or wherever she and the triplets were. He might be harried and tired, but his children came first. She hadn't seen his devotion at first. Now she did.

She also saw how badly his ex-wife had wounded him. "Want to talk about her?"

"No." He tipped his head to one side, his expression sad. "But maybe I need to so you won't hate me for being such a jerk."

As if that could ever happen.

"You must have loved her very much." Saying the words caused a pinch in her chest, but she was nothing if not a good friend.

"I did."

His admission hurt worse, so she reminded herself again that they were friends, and she was a summer employee.

It didn't help much.

"Sabrina was a head-turner," he said. "I fell like a boulder the first time I saw her. Thought she felt the same."

He rubbed a hand over his five o'clock shadow. The whiskers made soft scratchy sounds.

Kyra steeled herself against the surge of attraction. Scruff and blue eyes had a powerful effect on her.

"Everything seemed fine at first. Sabrina claimed to adore cowboys, wanted to live on a ranch and own horses. She loved showing me off to her city friends, like some kind of new toy." His laugh was bitter. "This cowboy was too dumb to see the truth. Her idea of ranch life was nothing more than a TV fantasy, a romantic notion. Glitz and glamour and doting cowboys. That's what she wanted. She got me instead."

Lucky girl.

Kyra stretched a hand across the small table. He twined his fingers with hers. They were cool and damp from the soda glass.

"I thought we could work things out. Thought she'd settle in and be happy. Right away, she got pregnant. I was thrilled. She was not."

The sadness in his eyes tore at Kyra. He was a man who'd dote on a pregnant wife and be proud of the babies—his babies—growing under her heart.

"What did she do?"

"Avoided me like the plague. And shopped. Retail

therapy, she called it. Buying new clothes, decorating the nursery, ordering baby items. I didn't care."

"You just wanted her to be happy."

His head bobbed. "It didn't work. She stayed gone all hours, *shopping*." He put the word in air quotes. "Sometimes overnight. Once for four days. I wanted to believe her, so I did. Anytime she was home, she was angry. At me, of course. I refused to see the truth. Blamed her moods on hormones. Stupid me."

"What happened?" Kyra kept her voice low, praying silently. Longing to understand this man better, to help him heal the wound his ex-wife had left behind.

He'd comforted her during the storm. She could do the same for him.

"Our marriage imploded. When she learned we were having twins, she had a fit, cried and screamed and blamed me for ruining her life." He looked toward his reflection in the darkened window, eyes glazed as if reliving the ugly moment. "If I thought she was going to be some barefoot, pregnant hillbilly stuck out in the sticks with a dozen snot-nosed kids, I was sadly mistaken."

Kyra sucked in a gasp. "That's horrible. I can't fathom anyone saying such a cruel thing."

"Such was her attitude about Sundown Valley and the Sundown Ranch. And me." In an aching voice, he said, "The next day she announced she was getting a divorce."

Kyra's sympathetic heart bled. For Wade. For the triplets. For a woman who did not know how to count her blessings.

"You must have been devastated." Sabrina had taken what should have been the most bonding time of their marriage and used it to emasculate her husband.

"Yeah. I was already reeling with the news that I was about to be a double daddy, and then my wife wants a divorce. I argued with her, reasoned with her, begged her to reconsider. For the sake of the babies."

He made a small cheerless sound of self-derision.

"Humiliating. But she finally agreed, after I offered her a lot of money, to stay until the pregnancy was over."

With a shudder, he reached for his Coke but didn't drink.

Kyra's gut twisted, aching for all he'd been through.

What kind of woman did that to the man she'd promised to love forever?

"Was she a Christian?" She knew the answer before he replied.

"That was my first mistake. I knew better, had been taught not to even date a nonbeliever. Sometimes a woman makes a man stupid. Anyway, I was."

"Not stupid. In love."

He patted her hand. "Thanks for that. But stupid fits better."

They exchanged a tiny smile, though his was sad.

"What happened when the babies were born? I guess she didn't change her mind?"

"Not hardly. They were delivered C-section, which infuriated her. Scars and stretch marks, you see. They were my fault. The babies were my fault. The C-section was my fault. Being stuck out here in the middle of nowhere was my fault. I'd ruined her life, and she wanted out."

Kyra squeezed his fingers, offering what little comfort she could.

"To add insult to what she viewed as a disaster," Wade went on, "we had three babies instead of two." He shook his head, his mouth drooping. "They were tiny and helpless and beautiful. I couldn't understand why she was angry."

"You loved them."

"Instantly. Fiercely."

Yes, fiercely. That's exactly how he loved them now.

"And Sabrina?"

"I pray they never learn of her reaction." His shook his head, slow and disbelieving. "Refused to touch them. I practically had to drag her to the NICU window to look at them. Which only happened once. The doc said she was suffering from postpartum depression, but I never believed that…"

A sick feeling tightened Kyra's stomach. "You still loved her."

"She was my wife. I took my vows very seriously. I'd promised to always love and cherish her. Do you know how a man feels when a woman rejects everything he is, including their children?"

"I can't imagine." But she could hear his bitterness and heartache.

"I'm a Christian, or try to be." He tapped his temple. "In my head, I understand that my feelings toward her, toward women in general, are wrong, but I can't stop resenting what she did. Especially to our babies."

Toward all women. Toward her, too.

He made a harsh, self-derisive sound. "You should have seen me when I first brought the triplets home from the hospital. What a disaster."

"What about Sabrina?"

"She'd had a C-section, so I understood at first why she kept to herself and claimed to be resting. But after I brought the babies home, I thought things would be different. That she'd change her mind about the divorce. About the triplets. She didn't. She stayed on the phone, making plans for the divorce and her new life."

While the old life needed her more than ever.

"Having kids was my idea, she said, so I could very well take care of them." Wade ran a hand over his face. "I still can't accept that she did that. How could she? But she did. So I moved into the nursery to look after the babies."

"How could you sleep?"

"I didn't. I was too worried about those tiny infants. Scared of doing the wrong thing, of hurting one of them. Sleep wasn't as important as watching them breathe." He huffed. "But then, I hadn't slept much since Sabrina made her divorce announcement."

"Alone with three newborns," she mused, barely able to take in how shattered and unnerved he must have been.

"Yes, scared out of my mind. They were needy and tiny, and I knew less about babies than I do astrophysics." He shook his head. "Bowie's great with horses, but babies scared him as much as they did me."

"So you hired Janey."

"Eventually. Thank the Lord for Janey." His mouth twisted. "The triplets should have had a mother to love them. Instead, I have to hire people to do what she should have done naturally. Turns out she'd reconnected with an old boyfriend during her so-called shopping trips, and he didn't want another man's kids."

Kyra would have done or said about anything just then to spare him the pain of her betrayal. No wonder he was bitter.

"Sabrina made a terrible choice that hurt you, hurt your children and hurt her, too, Wade, though, she may not realize it yet. She needs our prayers."

He extracted his hand from hers. She felt the disconnect as his anger returned. Nearly two years had passed, but Wade was far from over his ex-wife.

"She deserves to be hurt." He closed his eyes, head down. "That's wrong. I know it is. God forgive me."

"He will. But you have to forgive Sabrina, too."

"Not possible."

She reached for his hand again, hoping, praying he'd receive her touch as a compassionate friend. "Only God can heal wounds as deep as yours, and He will, if you'll let Him."

He lifted his head, looking at her from beneath hooded eyes. "Is that what your dad would say?"

Her lips tilted a tiny bit. "Yes. And he'd give me a dozen scriptures to go with his advice."

"Such as?"

"'Come unto Me, all ye that labor and are heavy laden, and I will give you rest' is a good one. I know it sounds like a trite platitude right now. It did for me at first, too."

"And now?"

"Now, I know He's the only way to ever be truly, fully healed and whole again. When I struggled with guilt over Tristan's death, His promises gave me comfort. And when I was afraid I'd never walk again, His peace settled over me like a hug. I can't explain it. But I know it's real."

She was still healing, both physically and emotionally, but she'd made great progress here in the quiet country with the mountains around her and with children to love.

Eyes widened, Wade tilted back in his chair. "They thought you wouldn't walk? That you'd be paralyzed? Why didn't you tell me that?"

Lots of reasons. One, he wouldn't have hired her to tote around his triplets. Two, it hurt to remember how terrified she'd been. Three, the long months of rehab were not cheerful dinner conversation.

"You have enough to worry about." She took a sip of Coke, the fizzy jolt burning her throat, washing down the memories.

"Uh-uh. No deal." He waved off her dismissal. "You listened to my pathetic tale, and you've lived through an even worse ordeal. Tell me."

Kyra inhaled a deep lungful of country air and put on a perky face. She was thankful to be alive. The year of recovery didn't matter anymore.

"I guess the worst part was not knowing the outcome. I'd lie in the hospital bed, put back together with plates and pins and super glue and wonder what it would be like to spend the rest of my life in a wheelchair." She widened her eyes at the joke, intentionally breaking the somber mood. "Maybe not super glue."

His eyes lit with humor. "It's pretty amazing stuff."

"That and duct tape." Again, an intentional joke, though a spot beneath her breastbone throbbed with painful remembrance.

She told the story quickly, hitting only the high spots. They'd had enough drama for one Fourth of July.

"All we could do was wait and see if my spine would heal. And that was up to God. Apparently, He was teaching me patience." She wrinkled her nose. "Waiting is not my forte."

"I had no idea. I'd never have guessed you'd been that badly injured." Blue eyes roamed over her appreciatively. "You look great. Really great."

Her neck warmed. To hide the flush of pleasure, she dipped her head and fluttered her eyelashes, teasing.

"Thank you, kind sir."

"I'm serious, Kyra. This paints an entirely new picture. Are you sure the triplets aren't too much for you?"

"Oh, no, no. I'm fine now. The physical therapy fixed me right up."

Physical therapy included painful months of regaining lost motor skills and learning to stand on her own two feet. Literally. But she wouldn't share the ugly details with Wade. Not tonight.

"Best of all, during that time, Jesus became my best friend. I learned to trust and lean on Him as never before."

"You do that well. You inspire me to be a better Christian."

Kyra let the comment slide by. Trusting Jesus was a

daily walk, a need to grow in her relationship with Him. She'd begun the journey, but she had a long ways to go. She was no one's model Christian.

"With God's help, here I am. Well and healed and chasing triplets every day. God's been good to me."

His fingers squeezed hers. "Is the injury why you stopped teaching?"

He seemed determined to know all her secrets.

She sobered. Sighed. He might as well hear the rest.

"The long recovery period was part of the reason I stopped teaching, but also the PTSD. I've been afraid even of going into a school building. I had panic attacks at the thought of something happening to one of my students again." Her mouth twisted. "So much for trusting Jesus, huh?"

"Was that why you were reluctant to take the nanny job?"

She nodded. "But I strongly believed God was leading me here. At first, I thought it was because the babies needed me, that I could help you."

He gave a soft, derisive laugh. "You were right about that."

"Maybe, but this summer was for me, too. I've healed, mentally and physically, and I'm confident I can teach again in the fall."

She'd not had a single flashback, not even on the day of the storm when she'd been frightened for the triplets.

His nod was slow and serious, but something flickered in his eyes, a disturbance of some sorts. "Any school would be fortunate to have you in the classroom."

"I hope so. I've lived in limbo too long already."

A tick of time passed. Slowly Wade extracted his hand and rose from the table. "It's late. I've kept you up too long. I should go."

She didn't want him to leave, but she followed him to

the door and stepped out onto the porch. Tonight they'd turned a corner by sharing their deepest wounds. She felt closer to him.

Did he feel the same?

He stopped at the porch's edge near a post and turned toward her. "Thanks for listening. Keep praying for me, and I'll do the same for you. Okay?"

She tipped her head to one side. "How do you know I do?"

"Because I know you. You're a good woman, Kyra. Special." He swallowed and the sound was loud in the country quiet. "Knowing you has been—" He didn't finish the thought. "I'm glad you chose to spend your summer with the Trudeau gang at the Sundown Ranch."

"Me, too." She tried to keep her voice light. And failed. "I've grown very fond of the Trudeau gang."

Very, very fond.

"Yeah?" He stepped closer, and in the next instant, she was in his arms. Kyra wasn't sure who'd made the first move and she didn't care.

When she lifted her face, his lips found hers and she melted into him. The kiss was nothing like that first brief kiss of comfort.

This was real. A man and a woman, two hearts thudding against each other, a swarm of emotions.

Time stopped. The pulsating night beat around them. Somewhere in the distance, a Roman candle boomed, and it was as if the fireworks sparkled behind her eyes in a kaleidoscope of color.

With the summer smells and sounds and the faintest remnants of Wade's manly aftershave swirling through her senses, Kyra's knees trembled a smidgeon. Her pulse went all fluttery, like tiny butterfly wings beneath her skin.

Every sense heightened, Kyra was aware of each place they touched, of the beat of his heart against hers, of his strong, tender hands in her hair, against the sensitive flesh of her neck.

She focused on how soft Wade's mouth felt against hers, felt his controlled passion and adored him all the more for it.

He held her close, but respectfully, his hands moving with tenderness against her back.

She'd been kissed before, but this was different. This was magnificent. She felt cherished and beautiful.

And she never wanted it to end.

He had to stop this craziness. Kissing Kyra was not on the agenda.

Not five minutes ago, she'd reiterated her plan to return to Tulsa.

Oh, but holding her, kissing her felt so right. She fit in his arms as if she were the missing piece to his broken puzzle.

He didn't want to let her go.

Reluctantly, he ended the kiss with a sigh. Kyra laid her head against his chest, saying nothing, but not moving away.

She made him feel like a man again. Worthy. Desirable.

He hadn't felt that way since his disastrous honeymoon.

Maybe that was why she'd let him kiss her.

Kyra had a tender, compassionate heart. She pitied him.

He shouldn't take advantage of her kindness.

"I'm sorry," he muttered, though he didn't realize he'd spoken out loud until she stepped away from him. "I shouldn't have done that."

In the shadowy darkness, he couldn't read her expression. "It was only a kiss."

It hadn't felt that way to him. But when had he ever read a woman's signals correctly?

She'd casually brushed off the best kiss of his life as nothing. And her reaction hurt. Crushed him, to be honest. Which was about as dumb as kissing her had been.

But he'd felt so close to her. She'd listened, letting him unload his bitterness without judging or turning away.

He'd do anything to maintain that friendly, warm, accepting relationship, even if it meant never kissing her again.

"The employer-employee thing," he said. Such a lame, untrue excuse. "I had no business stepping over that line."

She crossed her arms and turned her face up toward the sky.

He wanted her eyes back on him. Wanted her hands on his shoulders, in his hair. Wanted her in his arms.

Where she should *not* be.

"Don't worry about it, Wade. I'll see you in the morning."

She was dismissing him, sending him home. Rightfully so. If he stood on this porch two more minutes, he'd say something stupid. Like, I love you.

Which was impossible, given the length of time they'd known each other.

"Right. Okay. Good night, then."

Fearing he was about to make a fool of himself, Wade stepped off the porch and strode toward the main house without looking back.

Chapter Twelve

Several awkward days passed in which Kyra wasn't sure what to say to Wade, and he avoided her with the excuse that the ranch was super busy. When they had a spare moment, he was cordial, thoughtful, polite, but he seemed to regret their conversation and that spectacular kiss. She didn't mention it, either, though she wanted to.

Something brewed between them, too strong to deny, though Wade was doing a real good job of the denial thing.

Haying season, he claimed, kept him in the fields from dawn until after dark.

This, at least, was true, but she missed their conversations, the times of teasing and sharing their day over the supper table.

Finally, late one night, their camaraderie returned as suddenly as it had fled. She wished out loud for a bowl of chocolate ice cream, and as tired as he had to be from a long day in the hay field, he'd gotten into his truck and driven to town, returning with a half gallon.

They ate ice cream together at the kitchen bar while he shared the woes of equipment failure during haying season and she told him about the T-ball game she and the triplets had played.

All three babies could hit the ball with the plastic bat and run on short chubby legs around the yard, yelling at the top of their lungs. They'd tumble and fall and jump up and run to her for a hug or a kiss or a high five.

It was adorable.

Wade had beamed with pride, looking, more than once, at the photos and videos she'd made.

The conversation had segued to other topics—her hobbies of biking and writing poetry, his surprising love of history and books. When she'd told him about belonging to a tap-dancing troupe at one time, he'd insisted she demonstrate.

But though they were friends again, he behaved as if they'd never been in each other's arms while she yearned for the sweet intimacy again.

Days melted into weeks and as the dates changed on her cell phone, she wanted to push back time. As much as she desired to teach again, she loved these precious children and cared deeply for their dad.

If the *love* word lingered in her heart, she didn't fight it. To her way of thinking, loving another was a beautiful thing, whether he returned the feelings or not.

But, oh, if only he could let go and see where their relationship might take them.

She prayed for him, as she'd promised, wanting only the best for him. Praying that his broken heart would someday heal, and he'd be free to love someone again. Even if that someone wasn't her.

Most nights, he and Bowie would come in after dark, covered in dust and bits of hay, so weary they could barely put one foot in front of the other.

Kyra had never realized what hard work went into running a successful cattle ranch.

Bowie would eat his dinner from the microwave and disappear. Sometimes he'd drive into town. Sometimes he'd head to his workshop. Mostly, he'd retire to his end of the rambling ranch and not be seen again until morning.

Wade invariably went to the nursery and stood over the cribs for a while, watching his triplets sleep.

His devotion tugged her heartstrings.

Fierce love, he'd said.

Toward the end of July, Kyra updated her résumé and, with a reluctance that troubled her, filed applications with several choice schools in her Tulsa suburb. Classes began in August. She couldn't wait around forever to make a decision.

Wade hadn't asked her to stay on as nanny. She couldn't stay anyway, not when she fell more in love with him every day, and he didn't return the feelings. The situation would prove too awkward.

Wade had received a few nanny applications from the employment office. Mothers wanting a day job when their kids started back to school. Every time he brought up the subject, she tensed, afraid this applicant was the one.

So far, none suited him, but someone would soon.

Her summer in the Kiamichi was nearly over.

All these thoughts rolled through Kyra's head one afternoon as she drove home from a quick milk-and-diaper run while Wade played with the triplets.

The day was scalding hot and bone dry, the sun relentless. Such was summer in Oklahoma, even here in the old rolling mountains she loved so dearly.

Dust rose in clouds from the graveled road, and a fat green grasshopper rode her unused wiper blades. Miles of wildflowers, yellow, orange and white, bloomed along the roadside.

She'd miss this. So much. But not as much as she'd miss the man and his babies.

Yet, this was the way things had to be. Her life was in Tulsa. His was here. City and country. He'd said as much at least a dozen times, letting her know his feelings in subtle ways.

She pulled off the road to pick Indian paintbrush and wild black-eyed Susans, the red and yellow color combination a cheer to her spirit and a pretty addition to tonight's dinner table. Butterflies flitted over the blossoms.

She drew in a breath of fresh-scented country air. Even in the heat, the air smelled good.

A splash of red caught her eye. She smiled at the cardinal and said a quiet "Thank You, Lord."

She'd seen them everywhere this summer, as if God wanted her to think of Him, of her mom, of Tristan.

Thinking of Tristan was bittersweet now, the sweet a new occurrence and evidence of her healing.

Back in the air-conditioned Spark, she turned up K-Love radio and headed home.

Home.

But not for much longer.

Rounding a curve near pasture four of the Sundown, she spotted a red pickup parked at the gate. Attached to the truck was a stock trailer.

She didn't know much about ranching, but she knew no one except the Trudeaus had any business on Sundown land. Especially with a trailer backed to the fence.

Tensing, worry slithering along her nerve endings, Kyra slowed for a good look, recognizing the truck and the barrel-chested man. Bud Keno. The neighbor with the filthy mouth who was suing Wade.

What was he doing on Trudeau property? Why had he backed a stock trailer close to the gate?

Even a city girl suspected he was up to no good.

Without considering the danger, Kyra wheeled into the turnout next to Keno's truck.

"Excuse me, sir." She leaned out her window. "May I help you? This is private property."

The red-faced man looked up, smirked, then blatantly cut the lock and shoved the gate open.

Several cows mooed and ambled toward the opening.

Shocked, Kyra slammed the car in Park and hopped out. "What are you doing? You can't do that!"

He glared at her, one hand on the open gate. "Mind your own business."

Kyra's pulse kicked into overdrive. Was the man trying to steal Wade's cattle? "This is my business. It's Trudeau land. You're trespassing."

Keno shoved off the fence and stalked in her direction.

Kyra backed up a step, fumbling in her short's pocket for her cell phone. A shiver of fear replaced the indignant concern.

"You need to leave right now."

Her voice sounded squeaky and scared. Fear roared in her ears.

The man stomped closer, jaw set and eyes bulged. Sweat stained his shirt.

He grabbed her upper arms and squeezed hard. She jerked against his grip. Big and bulky, he didn't budge.

"You're fixing to get yourself hurt, lady." Teeth clenched, spittle gathered in the corners of his mouth. "Get gone before I forget my manners."

With a powerful shove, he sent her flying backward. She stumbled and fell, landing hard. Pain shot up her vertebrae. Gravel dug into her elbows.

Keno snorted a cruel laugh, the ugliest sound she'd ever heard.

"Jesus, I need You." Her breath short and shaky, the prayer came unbidden as Kyra scrambled to open the screen on her phone. Her fingers shook.

If the man was stealing cattle, Wade needed to know what was happening.

And she needed help. She needed it now.

Before she could complete the call, Keno yanked the device from her hand and flung it across the road.

Kyra crab-crawled backward, seeking purchase against the slick gravel to get on her feet. The man was a maniac.

Adrenaline stoked, she grabbed a fence post, lurched to a stand and rushed across the road to find her phone.

"I know who you are," she yelled back at him, waving the broken phone as if it would work. "You won't get away with this."

Unless he killed her.

"God is my refuge, my ever-present help in a time of trouble. In Jesus's name, leave!"

Keno cursed and shied away as though she'd hit him. Then, muttering under his breath, he stormed to the red truck and roared away. Loose gravel pinged Kyra's legs and arms.

Weak and trembling, she hurried to close the gate, shooing the cows away from the opening. The big bovines weren't nearly as intimidating as the man.

Reaction began to set in. The adrenaline crash turned her legs to jelly.

All she could think of was getting home to Wade.

"Wade. Wade!"

Wade heard the fear in Kyra's voice and nearly broke his big toe rushing toward the sound. He'd been barefoot, taking a brief siesta while the triplets napped and Kyra went into town.

They met head-on in the hallway. Her face was as white as paper.

She fell against him.

Heart lurching, he caught her by the shoulders.

Fear gleamed from her eyes.

"What's wrong? What happened? Did you have a wreck?"

"Keno."

The name elicited a visceral response. His gut twisted. His blood began to heat.

"Keno? What did he do?" Wade heard the danger in his voice. "Did he hurt you? Are you hurt?"

He pushed her away to see for himself.

"Just my elbows." She turned her arms for his appraisal. They were scratched and bloody. "I fell."

"He pushed you?"

She nodded.

Wade's jaw tightened. "He will pay for this. If he wants me, I'm here, but touching you crosses the line. This ends now."

She put a finger to his lips. That sweet, precious finger trembled, inciting his rage all the more.

"I'm all right, Wade. Keno scared me, pushed me down and broke my phone, but I'm okay now that I'm home. But your cows—"

Wade sliced a hand against the air. "Forget the cows. He *hurt* you!"

"Thank heaven the babies weren't with me."

Leave it to Kyra to think of the babies before herself. She even considered his cows first.

Incredible woman.

"What happened? Tell me. Start at the beginning."

She did, but when she got to the part about Keno grabbing her, Wade thought his head might explode.

"You shouldn't have stopped. You should have driven past and called me."

"I know that now, but at the time, I saw his trailer backed close to the gate getting ready to steal your livelihood. I thought if I stopped and said something, I could scare him away. I never imagined he'd attack me."

"Well, imagine next time. Don't take chances." He sounded mad, but he wasn't. Not at her, anyway. Keno, on the other hand, was in his crosshairs. "We need to get those scrapes cleaned up."

"I will." She touched a reassuring hand to his shoulder. He wanted to grab it and hold on, afraid to let her out of his sight.

"Wade, I am all right. Stop fretting."

"Are you sure you don't need a doctor?" The thought of her injury, still healing, hit him like a brick. "Your back?"

"Jarred, sore, but ibuprofen should fix me up." She pointed toward the door. "Go see to your cattle."

She had to be kidding. "Keno's not stable, Kyra. Stay away from him at all costs. Next time, he might hurt you badly."

"Don't worry." Her head swung back and forth, one palm held outward. "I don't want another encounter with him."

"If anything would have happened to you, I don't know what I'd do. Something drastic probably." He was tired of turning the other cheek. He felt wild, dangerous, vengeful.

Kyra was a small, delicate lady, and no match for the burly rancher.

Her bravado scared him to pieces.

Giving in to an irrational need, he tugged her back into his arms. Every primal, overprotective cell in his body rushed to guard duty.

His lips grazed her soft flower-scented hair. She loved flowers.

"Are you sure you're okay?" The question was a whisper, spoken from a heart that had nearly shattered when she'd rushed into the house, calling his name.

"Yes."

He didn't want to leave her. She was hurt, regardless of her argument to the contrary. Her elbows leaked blood. Reminded him of her bloody fingers digging to save her students.

He shuddered.

"Thank God," Wade murmured over and over again, as if to reassure her when actually he was reassuring himself.

Kyra's head moved in agreement against his chest.

A slight tremor shivered through her body.

Still, he held her. And she let him.

His rage burned against any man who'd put his hands on a woman. Not just any woman, but on Kyra. Keno would pay for this.

When her trembles finally subsided, and while Wade struggled not to say something stupid, he led her to the couch and sat next to her, close in case she needed him.

She kept hold of his hand.

He liked the feeling. The need to protect swelled his chest, flamed in his heart.

"You need to check that gate, Wade," she insisted, "and make sure he doesn't return. He had a trailer."

"And you need to clean up those scrapes and call your doctor."

Her smile was tentative. "I will if you'll stop fretting over me and go."

"I'm not leaving you. Bowie can handle the cattle." He pointed toward the bathroom. "Antiseptic in the cabinet."

"I know." Pushing off the couch, she left the room.

Of course she did. She tended his and Bowie's ranch scrapes and cuts, as well as those of the babies.

Tended. Nurtured. Loved. Such was his Kyra.

Keno's actions today were the final straw.

He was done. *Done.*

Stewing, jaw tight, still trying to control the need to drive to Keno's ranch and pound his head into the ground, Wade texted Bowie.

After another minute, he called the sheriff. This time he was pressing charges. Enough was enough.

* * *

That night, for the first time in weeks, Kyra suffered a nightmare. Trapped beneath rubble with rain pouring in, Tristan calling her name and the babies crying, she struggled to reach her cell phone. Bud Keno stomped on her back and then on the phone, laughing, mocking her distress. Helpless, she pleaded for mercy, but the man walked away and left them to die.

She awoke with a start and sat up in bed, disoriented. Her heart thundered. Anxiety jacked through her veins.

She flung back the covers. Her legs were free. Could she move? Could she walk?

Swinging her feet to the floor, Kyra stood, relief flooding in with the sunlight, reminding her where she was.

Safe. Not trapped. Not paralyzed, though her back ached.

She stretched, hoping against injury from the fall. She didn't want Wade to worry. He'd been angry enough as it was. If he thought Keno had reinjured her back, he might do something crazy.

At his insistence, she'd used the office landline to phone her doctor since her cell phone was broken. The neurologist had given instruction to resume her physical therapy protocols and call him in a few days if the discomfort continued.

Both Wade and Bowie had convinced her to press charges against Keno for assault, and the sheriff had taken things a step further by opening an investigation into Keno's cattle operations.

She prayed for a resolution to the trouble between the two ranches. She prayed for quick healing of her back, too. Triplets taxed the healthiest body.

After dressing, Kyra crossed the dimly lit yard to start breakfast.

"Morning." Wade was already up, as usual, putting

bacon in the skillet. The man did love his bacon. "Kids are still down."

"They're sleeping later now."

A cute little grin made spokes around his eyes. "Praise the Lord."

"Where's Bowie? Still in bed?"

"Long gone. Gotta finish the south hay meadow today."

"He has to eat."

"Put a plate in the microwave. He'll eat later." He looked her over. "You okay? How's the back?"

He would have to ask. "A little stiff."

"Why don't you take off today? Rest. Take care of those elbows. I'll stay home and wrestle the triplets. You shouldn't be lifting."

She waved him off, then opened the fridge and took out a carton of eggs. "It's haying season. You're needed in the fields."

He paused, a spatula aloft. "Well, aren't you sounding like a rancher this morning?"

Unshaven, Wade's dark beard framed the supple lips she couldn't forget and brought out the intensity of his blue eyes. The effect was a little dangerous, a lot manly and so handsome she nearly lost her breath.

But looking was such a pleasure. "Pancakes or eggs?"

His eyebrows lifted, hopefully. "Both?"

With a snicker, she gave him a shoulder push and took out the pancake mix. "Someday I'll learn to make flapjacks from scratch."

"You don't hear me complaining."

Come to think of it, he never complained about anything. He was easy to be with, a good man. "Men will eat shoe leather and not complain."

"Only if you put gravy on it."

She laughed. "What put you in such a good mood this morning?"

"I'm not sure. Maybe pressing charges against Keno did the trick."

Maybe. But from her way of thinking, pressing charges was like waving a red cape at a horned bull. He'd only get angrier.

Wade's good mood lasted all morning even after the baler broke down and he'd had to come in for repairs. Once the baler was up and running, he popped into the house for a break to see the triplets, and if he were honest, to see the nanny.

He worried about her, especially after yesterday.

What she'd done had shaken him to the core. But he also thought she was the bravest woman in the world. His petite little nanny going mano a mano with a bully like Keno to protect Trudeau property. *His* property.

He shook his head as he wandered through the rambling house in search of her.

She was still recovering from that horrific tornado, another incredible act of bravery on her part. The thought of her trapped beneath a school building with dying children nearly brought him to his knees.

More than a year's recovery. He couldn't fathom such strength, such courage in so small a woman.

Keno, blast his eyes, could have caused more injury, setting back her recovery for months.

This morning, Wade couldn't get that out of his mind. He fretted, wanting to be with her, to be sure she and the babies were okay.

Logically, he knew they were. The primal male in him had to verify.

He found them in the den. They were busy and didn't notice him at first, so he simply watched and enjoyed, his heart too full to speak.

Kyra sat in the middle of the floor surrounded by toys

and toddlers. Behind her was a basket of folded clothes and a notebook. He'd noticed how she scribbled poems and milestones in her free time, such as it was.

Maybe he should give her more time off. To enjoy herself, preferably with him.

But who would watch the babies?

As he mulled the dilemma, kiddie songs played in the background. Abby and Ben stacked blocks and knocked them down, cackling with each destruction. Caden spun in circles, clapping his hands and singing gibberish to the music.

On one half-turn, Caden spotted Wade and yelled, "Dad!"

On chubby legs, his boy ran to him and stuck his head between Wade's grass-flecked knees. Chest filled with love, Wade flipped the baby upside down, relishing the gurgle of laughter.

The other two left their toys to get in on the game, and he spent the next few minutes flipping kids upside down, then slowly pulling them to his chest for an upside down hug and a loud smacking kiss.

Kyra remained where she was, a soft smile on her face. She was so pretty, so serene and calm with his babies. Most of all, she was loving. Could another nanny ever take her place?

In the midst of this controlled chaos, his phone rang. With a child clinging to each leg, he untangled himself. Kyra swooped in to distract the balls of energy while he stepped into the hallway to take the call.

Kyra could hear the low rumble of Wade's voice. He sounded serious. When he returned, he waded through the babies and said, "We need to talk."

A frown dented the space between his eyebrows.

"What's going on?"

"That was Keno's lawyer."

"Oh, no. What now?"

"He wants to make a deal. If we'll drop the assault charges, he'll drop his frivolous lawsuit."

"Then do it."

"He threatened you, Kyra. He shouldn't get away with that."

"Isn't dropping the silly lawsuit enough recompense?"

"Not in my book." He raked a hand through his hair. Already tousled from his hat, the light brown locks stood straight up. His lips formed a hard flat line. "But the decision isn't mine, Kyra. You're the injured party."

Kyra reached up and smoothed his hair. Standing close, he smelled of hay and outdoors with a hint of hardworking sweat. Strange how she could find manly sweat appealing.

"Make the deal, Wade." She spoke softly, her eyes on his blue, blue ones. "If you don't, he may get angrier and meaner than he already is. Dropping the charges could be the olive branch that brings peace between you two."

He stacked a fist on each hip and stared toward the toddlers who seemed to be everywhere at once.

"I don't like it."

"Have you prayed about it?"

"No. But I imagine you have." He exhaled a long frustrated breath. "Are you sure?"

"Positive. We have to try. Besides, you have enough on your plate without a frivolous lawsuit hanging over your head. I want that gone."

"Ah, Kyra." He reached out, cupped her face. "You're a special kind of woman."

"I want what's best for you, Wade. Always." The words were as close as she'd come to dumping her heart out on the family room floor.

"I want the same for you."

Though she didn't fully understand his meaning, her heart soared.

A beat of time, two thuds of her pulse, passed while they stared at each other. She longed for him to kiss her again, as he'd done weeks ago.

His gaze fell to her mouth, his tender rough palm still warm against her cheek.

He cared for her. She was convinced he did. Why couldn't he let go of the past and trust in love again?

Just when she thought he might, one of the babies howled and the moment was lost.

Aching, Kyra moved away from Wade's warm tempting person to stop Ben from whacking Abby with a block.

When she turned back, Wade had moved to the doorway. "Almost forgot something. Be right back."

He loped out of the room.

Running from his own emotions? Or running from her?

Probably both.

Flummoxed by his conflicting behavior, Kyra returned her attention to the babies, distracting Abby with a different toy. Ben was not about to give up his blocks.

Wade reentered the room. If the almost kiss was on his mind, he didn't show it.

"I had to run into town for a baler part and stopped at the cell phone store." He handed her a small box.

She opened it. Inside was a new smartphone.

"You didn't need to do this." But her heart sang with pleasure at his thoughtfulness.

He shrugged. "It's my fault yours is broken. You were protecting Trudeau property."

"Which was my choice."

He gave her a lopsided grin. "Come on, Kyra. Take the phone. The store clerk set it all up, imported your numbers and apps. You can change anything you like."

He shrugged. "Or return it for a different kind. Whatever you want."

You. I want you.

Kyra didn't say that, of course.

She ran her fingers over the dark shiny glass. "I don't know what to say. This is beyond thoughtful and generous…" *And caring.*

"Consider it a bonus."

"Oh. Right. A bonus. Okay." A shadow passed over her good mood.

Wade had promised a bonus if she cared for the babies until school started.

The expensive gift wasn't personal. It was business, payment for a job well done.

Wade watched as various emotions moved over Kyra's face. Her reaction wasn't what he'd expected. He'd wanted her to be thrilled. Truth was, he'd kind of expected her to throw her arms around his neck and snuggle up close the way she'd done yesterday.

Instead, she stared at the phone, unsmiling, as if she were disappointed.

"If you want a different brand—"

She shook her head. "The phone is perfect, Wade. Thank you."

Then why wasn't she beaming with pleasure? Why did she look sad?

He'd never understand women.

Wade grabbed his hat from an end table. Boots shuffling like an awkward adolescent, he said, "Guess I'll get back to work."

Unless she asked him to stay.

When she didn't say a word, he turned on his boot heels, crammed his hat down on his hard head and walked out.

Chapter Thirteen

An uneasy truce hovered over the ranch in the days following the incident and the dropped charges. No more gates left open or fences cut. No more creeks dammed up. No more threats and ugly phone calls.

Dare he hope the feud was over?

After generations of animosity, Wade wasn't counting on it.

But peace with the Keno bunch wasn't the only thing weighing on Wade's mind.

His real trouble was Kyra. He thought about her constantly, though he chalked this behavior up to concern about her well-being. He didn't trust Keno as far as he could toss a tractor.

He also felt responsible for her injury. She seemed fine. Her elbows healed, and she denied any further back pain. Thank the Lord. She'd had enough pain in her life.

Her odd behavior on the day he'd given her the phone still played in his head like a bad movie. He'd wanted to kiss her, to hold her, to make her happy, none of which made a lick of sense.

The fact that he texted her several times a day to be sure she and the babies were safe wasn't lost on him, nor on his cousin, Bowie. The quiet cowboy didn't say much with his words, but his looks spoke a whole dictionary.

Inside barn one, the scent of horse sweat and freshly mucked stalls rose with the day's heat.

Holding his smartphone in one gloved hand, Wade scowled at his cousin. "What?"

Bowie shrugged and went back to grooming his bay gelding.

"She can't even ride a horse," Wade said, certain he read Bowie's mind.

Bowie smirked. "Teach her."

He could ask again. Maybe, now that she knew him better, she'd trust him to teach her, to keep her from harm.

He stared at the phone screen for a full minute, awaiting her reply. When nothing happened, he shoved the device in his back pocket and said, "Call it a day. I'm going to the house."

Bowie's quiet laugh followed him all the way to the kitchen where Kyra, with the triplets spread around the floor like moving rugs, was stirring chicken and rice in the Crock-Pot.

The woman had more Crock-Pot recipes than he knew existed. He'd have to ask where she got them before she left.

Which he didn't like to think about.

He yanked his hat off. "Hey."

She turned away from the counter with a smile. "Hey yourself. You look hot."

Was that a blush he spotted? Did she think he was hot in the attraction department?

Yeah, he thought maybe she did. She wasn't the kind of woman to go around hugging and kissing guys without a real good reason. And that one spectacular kiss on the Fourth of July lingered in his mind, delicious and tempting.

Except she was the nanny.

"Want some tea? Freshly made."

He stared at her, contemplating the woman, recalling that kiss, considering all the ways she'd made his life easier. Better.

Without waiting for his answer, she filled a glass with ice and poured the amber liquid.

He loved iced tea, and she knew it. So did she. It was one of the many things they had in common. His was sweet. Hers unsweetened with lemon, and she always had a thermal cup by her side. Lidded, naturally. Otherwise, one of the kids would upend it.

"Thanks." He swallowed a cold drink and wiped his mouth with the back of his hand. "I was thinking. Weather's cooled off, but it won't last long. After dinner, let's take the babies for a stroll. I want to show you something."

She looked at him for a long moment as if gauging his intent. Well, he didn't know his intent. He only knew he wanted to spend more time with her.

Probably to make sure she was safe and happy.

Yeah, that.

She nodded. "Sounds fun."

Suddenly, his mood went from okay to terrific. He grabbed a baby and two-stepped around the kitchen while Kyra smiled, and Wade wished she were the one in his arms.

"Baby kittens?" With the triplets secure in their triple stroller, Kyra fell to her knees on the soft hay inside barn one. "Oh, Wade, they're gorgeous."

When they'd started their evening stroll, a request that delighted her, Wade had taken them directly to the barn for a surprise.

"I thought you'd like them." His expression was

pleased, his eyes sparkling with gentle humor. "Not big and scary like horses, huh?"

He knelt, too, and picked up a mewling orange kitten, handing it to Kyra. Barely opened eyes blinked at her.

The six kittens of all colors and patterns had round, full bellies. Each time one of them moved, the mama cat nudged her baby back into place and gave it a good lick.

"Horses and cows don't seem so scary anymore."

"No?" Wade's head swiveled toward her. "Think you might reconsider my offer of riding lessons?"

Smiling, Kyra snuggled the furry baby close to her face, but didn't respond to the invitation. She'd love to learn to ride with him, but unless something changed quickly, she wouldn't be here long enough to begin.

Especially after today's phone call. The trajectory of her life seemed to be taking a path away from Sundown Ranch and back to Tulsa.

She'd been praying for God's will. Was this it?

She should tell Wade about the call.

How would he react?

She snuggled the kitten closer, relishing the beauty of new life, new beginnings.

And yet, she didn't know if the next new beginning was the one she truly desired.

With a tenderness that belied his strength, Wade stroked between the mama cat's ears. "You're doing good, little mama."

The pretty calico blinked large yellow eyes, watchful but trusting of the man who fed and cared for her.

A man to trust. A man of integrity. A man with deep scars that held her at arm's length.

Except when he didn't.

So confusing.

The triplets, upon seeing the barn cats, began their usual demands to get out of the stroller.

"Not happening, kids," Wade said. "Kittens are delicate and you might accidentally hurt them. Daddy will help you hold one, but you have to be super gentle. Okay?"

Three heads nodded, eyes wide and fascinated.

"Are these their first kittens?"

"Yep."

Side by side, their shoulders touching, they showed the children how to stroke the kittens. Kyra used her quiet coaxing voice, and each child proved surprisingly gentle. Even Ben controlled his boisterous impulse.

"They're such good kids, Wade." On their first meeting, she'd never imagined how much the rancher had put into training and caring for his children. No wonder he'd been frazzled.

"You have a lot to do with that."

"So do you. Kids this age learn fast and want to please. Guiding them in the right direction isn't rocket science, but it takes time and thought. You obviously gave them that long before I came into the picture."

"Takes lots of patience and love, too." He placed the kittens back with their mother and pulled Kyra to a stand. "You have both those in spades."

"Lying in a bed for months doesn't give a person much choice. Learn patience or be miserable."

"You chose patience."

"Trust me, it wasn't easy. I prayed a lot, and that's the only thing that kept me sane."

"Which is one of the things I find so admirable about you. Prayer first. I sometimes forget how crucial God is to every single day of my life. Of my children's lives."

His strong hands, gentle with the kittens, took hold of her bare upper arms with the same tenderness.

They stood facing one another, the triplets squirming and pounding their respective toys against the stroller, the kittens quietly mewing. In a nearby stall, a horse whickered, his hoof bumping the sheet iron wall.

It would be so easy to blurt out her feelings, to admit she'd fallen in love with him.

But what good would that do? He'd only feel guilty that he didn't feel the same. Affection, yes. Attraction, definitely. Even appreciation. But Wade was stuck in the past, and until he let go and forgave, he couldn't love again.

Because she cared, she wouldn't put him in an awkward position.

So she kept her thoughts to herself.

With a lightness of heart she didn't feel, she tiptoed up and kissed his cheek and took two steps back.

If she remained close, she might say something she shouldn't.

"Thank you for showing us the kittens." Kyra squeezed her hands together in front of her. "Now, I need to share something with you."

Wade blinked three times in an attempt to reorient. He'd been about to kiss the nanny. He'd decided the time was right and hoped maybe, just maybe, he could convince her to stay on long after the summer ended.

Which would happen any day now.

"Share something?" Her wording made him wary. "Are you okay? Your back?"

"My back is fine." She accepted an empty sippy cup from Caden and thanked him. The baby garbled, "Tank oo," and went back to the toys dangling from his section of the stroller.

"A school in Tulsa called me earlier today. We set up an interview."

Wade's heart stopped beating—he thought it had, anyway. An interview meant one thing. She was leaving. Soon.

He wasn't ready, and his reluctance had nothing to do with the fact that he had yet to approve a new nanny.

Tulsa might only be a few hours away, but it might as well be the moon. The babies were losing her. *He* was losing her.

He gulped back the cry of protest. Teaching was her dream, her calling. She'd told him as much from the start. He couldn't stand in her way.

If she wanted him and the babies, she'd say so.

Instead, she'd scheduled an interview.

"Is it a good school?" he managed. "A safe one?"

"Yes." She stepped behind the stroller and aimed it toward the outside. Baby legs kicked a pounding rhythm against the footrests. "Lincoln Elementary has a top-notch reputation and one of the best special-needs programs in the area. I'm fortunate to get an interview."

He held the barn door while she and the stroller passed through into the fading day.

"Don't sell yourself short. You're terrific. They'll snap you up like a dog on a cheeseburger."

How he could joke at a time like this amazed him. He wanted to fall in the dirt and kick like a disappointed child.

But he was a man. He'd been left behind before. He could do it again. At least, this time, the woman had been honest. They'd come into this with an agreement, and though his feelings had changed, hers hadn't. She liked him, loved his babies, but she would leave.

"To be honest, I'm nervous. I haven't been in a school building since the tornado."

Right. The tornado. Of course, it would be on her mind. "Worried about the flashbacks? You haven't had any, have you?"

"Just a bad dream one night, but I haven't been in a school building, either. I freaked out in the parking lot of Sundown Valley Elementary a few months ago and never went inside."

"You can do this now, Kyra." Somehow, with a prayer in his aching heart, Wade managed to say the words she needed to hear. "It's what you've worked toward for more than a year. The woman I've come to know is strong and resilient. God has not given you the spirit of fear, remember?"

Her lips curved. "Look at you tossing verses at me. And you're right, of course."

The stroller wheels crunched onto the gravel path surrounding the house and barns as casually as if this were an ordinary sunset stroll with the triplets.

As if they were two friends discussing the weather.

"God's words, not mine. Gotta be true." He winked, though his heart felt like it would come out of his chest.

Don't leave, don't leave, don't leave.

But she would. Returning to the classroom was her dream, her goal. He'd known that from the beginning.

She'd go back to Tulsa where she belonged.

He didn't want her to go. But he wanted her to be happy.

"Hey." He curved one hand over hers on the stroller bar, their sides bumping, their footsteps in sync. So much about them was in sync. All but the leaving.

"You can do this, Kyra. You're strong." *And beautiful*

and wonderful. "You're ready. You know you are. But if you need moral support, let me go with you."

He'd die a little in the doing, but, if she needed him, he wouldn't let her face her fears alone.

"No. You're right. I can do this."

Fighting the urge to stop the stroller and beg her to stay, Wade accepted the truth. She didn't need him. She didn't want him. "When?"

"Next Tuesday. If you don't mind, I'll switch days and work on Sunday. I love going to church with you and the babies, anyway."

"Sure thing." He tried to sound pleased. "Whatever you want to do. If you change your mind about that moral support, I'll drive you up on Tuesday."

She gave him a long searching look, then turned her head to look at the blazing sunset.

Had her eyes looked glassy?

Nah, he was imagining things.

This was what she wanted.

So it was what he wanted for her.

Chapter Fourteen

Pulse whacking her eardrums, Kyra smoothed her hair, straightened her summery white over-jacket and, with full skirt swirling around her knees, started the long walk up the sidewalk into Lincoln Elementary.

Dad's prayer moments before by phone bolstered her confidence. Her mind and body had healed. She could do this.

Inside the bag containing her document folder, her phone pinged a text message. Stepping under the shady, covered porch, she fished out the device.

I'm praying for you. You got this.

Kyra smiled through a sudden rush of moisture behind her eyes.

Wade. Thinking of her. Knowing the exact time she'd need his encouragement.

Her thumbs moved over the keyboard. I've arrived, about to go in the building. Feeling strong.

She sent the text, and a reply came almost immediately. You ARE strong. ABC send their love.

ABC, a shortcut for Abby, Ben and Caden.

The text closed with a silly strongman emoji intended to make her laugh.

With Wade's encouragement swirling in her thoughts, she pushed open the door and went inside.

The scent hit her first. The smell she'd always loved. Books and paper mingled with cleaner and the fresh paint of summertime updates. And that indefinable something that smelled like school.

She closed her eyes and fought off a sudden flash of memory, the sounds of falling bricks and ripping lumber. The cries of frightened, injured children.

Praying, seeking a place of peace, she paused in the hallway and focused on the entry bulletin boards, bright and colorful with welcome-back information.

Everything was intact. The building was secure.

There was nothing to fear.

She was firmly in reality.

As she made her way to the door marked Office, the jitters began to subside. Any residual anxiety was interview nerves, not PTSD.

Her palms were damp, her chest tight, but she was here, and, with God's help, she would be okay.

Drawing a deep cleansing breath, she turned the knob and stepped into the principal's office.

All through the interview with the principal and his selection team, Kyra's confidence grew. She fielded questions about the tragedy and her recovery, and even spoke of Tristan without breaking down.

She silently thanked Wade for that. He'd listened, letting her purge the ugly guilt and take a step closer to healing.

With every question and every answer, her thoughts strayed again and again to the Sundown Ranch, to Wade and his adorable triplets.

To the laughs they'd had, their shared pride in the babies' milestones, to the tender moments between them.

What a wonderful summer God had given her with Wade and his babies.

How could she bear to be away from them now that she loved them so?

Who would know about Abby's favorite blankie? Or Caden's need to be held and rocked before nap time? Who would have the patience to see past Ben's rambunctious nature to the kindhearted lovebug inside?

All these thoughts swirled while she answered a volley of questions and asked some of her own.

When the interview ended, she rose, clutching her folder. Like everything else, the folder reminded of her Wade, of their first meeting.

The principal stood, too, and as he did so, buttoned one button on his gray jacket. He was a friendly man, likely a fine principal. "Thank you for coming in today, Miss Mason."

"Thank you for the opportunity." Her gaze swept the other three people in the office. "I've enjoyed meeting you."

"You should know, we took the liberty of contacting references from your application before today. They are stellar." He smiled. "I think you'll be hearing from us soon."

She should be delighted, but all she could do was nod and say, "Thank you."

As Kyra exited the building and stepped into the August heat, waves of relief mixed with dread rolled through her.

She'd proven to herself that she could enter a school building, that she could teach again. "Thank you, Lord."

Now, she had to make a decision. What would be her answer if she was offered the position?

Wade checked his text messages a dozen times during the hour he knew Kyra was interviewing.

In between checking, he prayed for her, prayed to say all the right words, prayed to be an encouragement.

This was her dream, and he wanted it for her.

He re-pocketed the cell phone, replaced his work gloves and started shoveling again. They had a problem with the ranch's irrigation system, and the only way to find the stoppage was to dig.

Alfalfa without water wouldn't make much fodder.

Bowie tossed a shovelful of mud behind him. Sweat beaded his face. Scalding hot August was a lousy time to be digging anything. "If you love her, don't let her go."

"What am I supposed to do, kidnap her?"

Bowie's teeth gleamed in his dirty, sweaty face. "I knew it."

"Knew what?"

"You'd finally wake up and realize that Kyra and Sabrina are not the same. Growing up in the city doesn't mean she can't love the country. And the people in it."

Wade huffed and stabbed the shovel harder into the ground. "You do remember that she has a job interview today, right? In Tulsa."

"Have you told her how you feel?"

Mud flew behind him. "She's bound to know."

Bowie made a rude noise. "I give up. Women aren't worth the trouble, anyway."

Wade glowered. "Kyra's worth about anything."

Shaking his head, his cousin laughed, and it was the kind of laugh that said Wade was being an idiot.

He stomped hard on the shovel, driving it deep.

Was he being an idiot? Should he talk to Kyra, tell her how he felt, ask her to stay?

He shook his head.

If he cared about her feelings, he'd keep quiet and do what was best for her.

Or was that the coward in him, the man who feared getting his heart stomped again?

"If she wants to leave, who am I to stand in the way?"

His cell phone tinged. He shucked his leather gloves and grappled for the device. The message was from Kyra.

Everything went great. Thank you for your encouragement and prayers.

As he read her next words his heart tumbled to the drainage ditch at his feet.

He looked up at his cousin. "They've already offered her the position."

Kyra drove straight to her dad's church, though she had to wait a few minutes to see him, something she'd grown accustomed to as a preacher's kid. He was in a premarital counseling session.

While she waited, she'd shot Wade a text, telling him about the job offer. Then she reread his texts. All of them.

The last one twisted her heart.

You did it. Proud of you. ABC send big love.

Big love. The kind she wanted from him.

The pastor's office door opened and a young man and woman exited, holding hands.

The tender sight pinched her heart.

Her dad appeared behind them, saw her and waved. "Next."

It was their usual joke.

Inside the office, Kyra settled into a chair, unsure where to begin.

Dad got straight to the point. "How'd it go?"

"Good. Great, in fact."

"No issues this time?" His tone was relieved.

"A bit of jitter, but once the interview began I was fine, and they must have liked what they heard because they took a vote as soon as I left."

"And?"

"They offered me the job with a significant pay raise. It's a wonderful opportunity."

Her dad studied her, his discerning eyes looking deep. "Why don't you look thrilled?"

"I am." She pressed her lips together, then sighed. "But I don't know if this is the right decision."

"Why wouldn't it be?" Elbows on his desk, he steepled his fingers the way she'd seen him do a hundred times when he was listening. She loved that about her pastor-dad. He truly listened. "You're a teacher. It's a position you've wanted. Tulsa is your home."

"That's my issue, Dad. I'm not sure this is home any-more."

"Ah." The steepled fingers tapped, tapped, tapped. "Wade Trudeau?"

She nodded. Dad knew her well, and his advice meant the world.

"I think I love him, Dad."

"I suspected as much when you invited me down to meet him. He seems to be a good man."

"He is. But I'm not sure he returns my feelings. That's the confusing part. One minute, I think he does, and the next, I'm sure he doesn't."

"He hasn't said anything to encourage you?"

"Sometimes I think he's afraid to, that he's afraid of getting hurt again." She'd told him about Wade's ex-wife.

"That's understandable, all things considered. Trust lost is hard to regain."

"But what if it's not fear? Maybe he doesn't care for me the same way I care for him."

He threw up his hands. "Then, the man's a moron."

She laughed. "Oh, Dad. You're such a dad."

"I take that as a compliment. Any man who doesn't see that my daughter is worth more than rubies, as Proverbs says, qualifies as a moron." He raised one finger. "However, I perceive Wade's problem is exactly what you said—fear. He has those little ones to consider. For that reason alone, he must be extremely wise in his choice of a mate."

"I never thought about that. He's devoted to those kids. Naturally, he'd want what's best for them."

"From what you've told me of his ex-wife, the man is bound to have a load of insecurities, especially about romantic relationships. He made a mistake once. He fears making another, painfully aware that another wrong choice would further harm his children."

"But I'm their nanny. He's watched me care for them."

"As an employee."

"When I'm with the babies, I don't feel like an employee."

"And yet, as evidenced by the interview today, and the fact that the two of you agreed to a summer-only work arrangement, Wade may see you as temporary in his life, another woman destined to leave him and his kids."

Could that be the reason for the push-pull in his behavior toward her? "That's true, I guess. When he hired me, I agreed to a summer only."

"Consider this. Take off another semester. Continue to work for Wade and see where God leads."

"I've thought about that. Wade hasn't found anyone to take my place. But the dream teaching job at Lincoln won't wait."

"Let me ask you one question. Perhaps your answer will tell you what to do."

"Okay."

"If you knew Wade was in love with you, and if he asked you to stay, which would you choose, Sundown Ranch or Lincoln Elementary?"

The answer was easy. "Love, Dad. You taught me that. Silver and gold and ambition fade away, but love never fails."

"Yet, the problem remains. You still don't know how Wade feels."

"Exactly."

He leaned back in his chair, steepled fingers tapping together beneath his chin.

"Don't you owe it to yourself to find out?"

Wade prayed off and on most of the day. He prayed for Kyra, for himself, for the crazy feelings he had for her. Most of all, he prayed to the do the right thing for everyone concerned.

His babies were at stake here. He couldn't foul up and make another major mess.

"Lord, I want Your perfect will. Show me the way," he'd prayed. "And help me forgive Sabrina."

He didn't want to, but Kyra had convinced him that forgiveness was freedom. Without releasing his ex-wife to God, he'd never experience real peace.

And now, as he perused the nanny application lying on his office desk, he wondered if God had sent an answer to at least one of his prayers, even if it wasn't the one Wade wanted.

Across from him, holding Caden on her lap, sat a grandmotherly woman with warm brown eyes and a kind face. Lena Craddock, a nanny by profession. A woman in search of a new crop of children.

Abby and Ben explored the small office space as if they'd not been inside a hundred times. Frequently, they stopped playing to stare at the stranger, and every time she'd pause the conversation to focus on them.

Everything about her seemed right for the position.

Except she was all wrong.

"You nannied for Mayor and Mrs. Reinholt for fifteen years?" He knew the answer. He'd already spoken with both, as well as with one of the children, now grown. They praised her highly.

"I did, but Mandy and Jacob are both in college now. They don't need my services any longer."

"I see." The woman was perfect on paper and in references. From what he could tell in a brief meeting, she'd do a great job.

He continued the interview, asking question after question, his hopes sinking with every strong reply.

When she left, he promised to call her in a day or two with his decision.

But he had a bad feeling that the decision was already made. Kyra had gotten her dream job, and a new nanny had arrived at the perfect time.

Might as well accept the inevitable.

God had answered his prayer.

Chapter Fifteen

From the cool blue-and-white comfort of her old bedroom at Dad's house, Kyra propped on a fluffy mound of pillows and pondered the conversation with her father.

She owed it to herself and Wade to be open and honest about her feelings. Even if she ended up rejected and embarrassed, she'd leave knowing she'd tried, knowing that she left a legacy of love behind on Sundown Ranch.

But the ache of loss would remain a long time.

Taking her phone, she whispered a prayer and tapped Wade's number. When he didn't answer, she tried the ranch office.

On the third ring, Bowie answered.

"This is Kyra, Bowie. Is Wade home? I tried his cell."

"He's on the south pasture. No service out there."

She knew that. The mountains blocked cell signals on a large part of the ranch.

"Okay. I needed to talk to him about…something." Boy, was that ever lame.

"I'll ride out and get him."

"No, no. No need to do that. We can talk when I get back tonight." Although a phone conversation would be easier than a face-to-face rejection.

"How'd the interview go?"

"Great."

"Wade said they offered you the job."

"They did."

Bowie, who was normally short and to the point if he spoke at all, seemed inclined to chat this afternoon.

"So, you're leaving us?"

"I don't know, Bowie…" Her voice trailed off. "I just don't know."

"Ah." That one word said he knew. "He feels the same."

Her heart leaped. She gripped the phone tighter. "You think?"

"Trust me. I know. I'm the one he's driving crazy. Kyra this. Kyra that. Kyra loves the triplets." His voice became a singsong. "Kyra's a great cook. She's a terrific listener, so caring and genuine. Kyra can calm the sea and walk on water."

She laughed at the last. "Then why hasn't he said anything?"

"You gotta understand something about Wade. Sabrina did a number on his confidence, his manhood." He made a growling noise. "Woman ought not do to a man what she did to him. And her own kids."

The usually quiet cowboy rarely said anything, much less anything negative about someone else. Sabrina must have been a disaster. "I know. He told me."

"Then you should understand. He thinks he's not enough to keep you here. Thinks you're eager to get back to your life in Tulsa, to teach again. He wants the best for you, Kyra, and he'll not stand in your way if Tulsa's what you want."

"It isn't." She laughed lightly. "And those are more words than I've heard you say all summer."

She could practically hear him shrug. "Needed saying."

"I hope you're right."

"Come home. Talk to him. Find out for yourself."

Go home. To Wade.

And pray that Bowie knew his cousin as well as he claimed.

* * *

Three chubby-legged toddlers ran toward Kyra, squealing and jabbering as if she'd been gone for years instead of one day.

Her emotions seized up. She fought off the tears pushing behind her eyelids. Love for these three flowed over her in a tsunami.

Going to her knees, she received all three at once, the impact rocking her backward. She laughed and hugged, kissing each one, admiring the toy Caden had shown her a dozen times.

She breathed in their scent, a mix of apple juice and baby soap, loving everything about them, their sweetness, their orneriness, their unconditional love.

A pair of dusty brown Justin Roper boots appeared in her line of vision.

Her pulse jumped. The moment was now. She'd prayed all the way from Tulsa, asking God to give her the strength to say what was in her heart, regardless of the outcome.

She looked up into Wade's eyes. A gentle smile hovered there.

"They missed you." His chest rose on an inhale. "So did I."

The jiggling pulse became a hammer in her heart. "I missed them, too. All of you. Can we talk?"

He nodded, serious now, as she untangled herself from the triplets and stood.

"I knew they'd love you," he said.

"The babies? Babies are easy." What about you?

He shook his head. "I meant Lincoln Elementary."

"Oh. That. Wade, I—"

He waved her off. "You don't have to explain or apologize. I understand. We had a deal. When will you move out?"

Was he asking her to leave?

Benjamin wrapped his arms around her knees. Holding her.

How could she leave him? How could she leave any of them?

Her dad's words, mingled with Bowie's, filtered through the uncertainty.

You owe it to both of you to find out.

With trepidation and longing, she raised her eyes to Wade's and said, "I didn't accept the position."

Hope flared in Wade like a Roman candle. He tamped it back. Just because she didn't take the job didn't mean she was remaining at Sundown Ranch.

Trying to give her an out, he asked the easy question. "The PTSD?"

"No." She took a step toward him. "The ABC and W."

"What?" Hope surged again and shot to the ceiling, hovering there, waiting, waiting.

Was she saying what he thought she was saying?

"I love these three nuggets of yours," she admitted, using his nickname for the triplets. "I can't leave them."

Hope, that fragile thing, lost all its air and tumbled down.

It was the babies she loved, not him. Kyra wanted to remain their caregiver.

"I've already found another nanny," he managed.

Make the break. Make it clean and quick before he lost his resolve, dissolved at her feet and begged her to stay. "I won't need your services."

"Oh, Wade," her voice ached. "I don't want to be their nanny. I want to be their mother."

Kyra's words hung in the air, changing everything. If Bowie had been wrong, she'd just made a fool of herself. Wade would be embarrassed, but he'd be kind in his rejection.

Heat rose in her cheeks. Her mouth went dry. Her heart pounded hard enough to break a rib.

She watched the play of emotion across the rancher's face. Shock. Amazement. Uncertainty.

It was the uncertainty that scared her.

"Aren't you going to say anything?" she asked.

Wade's Adam's apple bobbed. His eyes never left hers.

Suddenly, as if a dam broke inside him, he groaned, took the final two steps to reach her and yanked her against his chest. She could hear his heart thundering as loudly as hers.

Against her hair, he murmured, his voice fierce with emotion, "I thought you wanted to leave. I wanted you to be happy. Don't leave. Please don't leave."

"No." Her hair rustled against his shirt. "No."

He tilted her back, holding her face between his strong cowboy hands, his eyes searching. Searching as if he could not believe what he was hearing.

"You'd choose me over your dream job in your hometown?"

"Always."

He tipped his head toward the ceiling. His chest rose and fell. "Ah, Kyra, my amazing Kyra. I think I loved you the moment you walked into my life and let Abby smear applesauce on your pretty dress, but I was convinced you'd go back to Tulsa."

"Maybe I wanted to at first, but then I fell in love with you. So many times you seemed to push me away. I wasn't sure you cared until I spoke to Bowie earlier today."

"Bowie?" He shook his head in wonder. "*He* told you?"

Kyra widened her eyes, as amazed as he. "In his own

succinct way, he said you loved me, but you thought I'd tire of the ranch life and leave the way Sabrina did."

"He's right. Exactly right."

"You weren't only safeguarding yourself. I understand that now. You were protecting the triplets. Your choices affect them, too."

With a relief in his expression that she'd never seen before, he nodded. "I don't want to tie you to something you'll despise in the long run. Your dreams are important."

"Yes, they are, and I'll teach again when I'm ready. But I can teach here in Sundown Valley, in this place that brings me such peace and joy. This ranch, these babies, *you* are my dream now. If you want me."

"Want you?" He lifted her chin. Wonder brightened his face. "Letting you go was about the hardest thing I could imagine. You fill a place in me that I thought was dead and buried. You give me hope. You build my faith."

At the beautiful words, emotion clogged the back of her throat.

As if he could see the tears she held inside, Wade's thumbs brushed the skin beneath her eyelashes, then slid down to stroke the corners of her mouth.

Tingles shimmered through Kyra's nerve endings.

"I need you, Kyra. You've brought light back into my life. I know I've been a hardhead, holding on to bitterness, fighting God, and you, every step of the way. I asked Him to forgive me. Will you?"

Jubilation bubbled up inside Kyra, a fountain filled with certainty. "Of course, I will. I do. I love you."

"Then please stay. Forever."

"Forever," she said, her lips closing in on his. "I like the sound of that."

Epilogue

One year later

"**D**on't say anything to Wade or Kyra. No need to worry them on their wedding day. We can check it out on our own."

Wade's ears perked up at Bowie's warning to Riley. The two men must be right outside the door to his dressing room.

He was pretty sure they weren't discussing the Keno problems, which had resurfaced with a vengeance about six months ago. That is, unless Keno was here at the wedding, waiting to cause a scene.

Nah, Kyra had picked an outdoor rustic-chic venue a few miles from the ranch. The chance of any of the Kenos knowing the exact location was slim.

The fact that his bride-to-be loved the outdoors and nature as much as he did still impressed and amazed him. During the past year, they'd hiked and fished and ridden horseback in this wilderness. And picnicked.

His mouth curved. Ah, those romantic picnics.

He'd truly met his match in Kyra Mason. Soon to be Kyra Trudeau.

Man, he liked the sound of that.

Wade grinned at his reflection in the mirror and straightened his mint-colored tie one last time. Mint, a color he'd never heard of until Kyra had chosen it as one of their wedding colors. He didn't care. If she liked it, so did he.

Opening the door to the dressing room, he found Bowie and Riley, as he suspected, standing outside. Behind them, in the beautifully decorated lodge where they'd hold their reception, friends and relatives gathered in clutches, filling the space with cheerful noise. White fairy lights above white-and-mint-laden tables added a silvery glow.

"Looking spiffy, cousin," Bowie said, tugging the sides of Wade's jacket together as if to cover the conversation he'd overheard.

As members of the wedding party, Bowie and Riley wore matching boots, gray vests, white dress shirts, mint ties and dark blue jeans. A carnation fluffy with mint and silver ribbons decorated their vests. Only Wade wore a jacket.

Bowie and Riley looked good, Wade thought, for a couple of old rough-hided cowboys.

The ever-hovering ache of loss tightened in his gut. Bowie and Riley shouldn't be his only attendants. Yates should be here. His best man. His only surviving brother.

Though he'd texted and called and left messages, his brother had, once again, shunned an important event in Wade's life.

It hurt.

Fighting off the sadness, he cut to the chase. "Tell me what's going on. Your voices came through the door."

"Nothing important. No big deal."

"Then tell me."

Bowie huffed, clearly unhappy that he'd overheard. "Some guy was lurking around near the edge of woods. When I spotted him, he ducked into the thick trees."

Wade stiffened. "Keno?"

Bowie shook his head. "Too thin to be Bill or Bud. Maybe one of the younger Kenos, but I don't think so."

His jaw tightened. "Describe him."

"Like I said, thin. About your height, maybe taller. Other than that, I don't know. He was too far away."

"Didn't you say he wore a ball cap pulled low?" Riley asked.

Bowie nodded. "Might have had a beard. He was in shadow so it's hard to say."

"Probably a vagrant hoping to score some free eats," Riley said, patting his flat belly. "I could smell that smoked meat all the way to my house."

Wade's lips twitched. They'd catered smoked ribs and chicken for the reception. "You're probably right. Nothing to worry about."

But he didn't like it.

Bowie put a hand on Wade's shoulder. "We'll keep our eyes peeled. You focus on marrying that fine woman of yours."

No use borrowing trouble. Whoever the guy was, he likely meant no harm. Marrying Kyra was the order of the day, not fretting over vagrants or Kenos.

His belly quivered with anticipation. He checked his watch. Today, he was taking a wife, the woman he should have waited for in the first place. Except he wouldn't have the ABCs, and those three toddlers were worth the pain of the past.

A clutch of Sundown Valley friends flooded into the lodge, including Becky and Shawna who would later serve the cake and punch. He couldn't be more pleased that Kyra had become close friends with the two women. Fact was she'd made so many friends in Sundown Valley their guest list was a mile long.

His friends spotted him with his groomsmen and came over to say hello.

After the usual congratulatory comments, the conversation moved to other topics.

At one point, Shawna, in her perky blond manner, said, "Did you hear the great news? Sage Walker is back in Sundown Valley. I don't know whether she's visiting or home to stay, but won't it be great to see her again?"

Beside him, Wade felt Bowie stiffen.

Wade slid a glance toward his cousin. The groomsman looked frozen in place, like a gray Popsicle in a mint tie. His jaw had gone rock-hard, his dark skin blanching. His mouth formed a straight line.

The conversation flowed on. No one else seemed to notice his cousin's odd reaction to the former resident's name, and Bowie didn't say anything, which wasn't unusual. But after that frozen moment, he pivoted abruptly and went inside the dressing room.

Wade frowned after him.

What was that all about?

He'd barely had time to wonder when Amy, Kyra's best friend and maid of honor, came his direction. Thick brown hair in long waves, she looked pretty in her gauzy, flowing mint dress.

"The bride wants to know if you're getting married today or want to wait until next October?"

Wade laughed. "Not a chance. Let's do this."

All thoughts of the mysterious stranger and Bowie's odd behavior fled as he thought of what would happen in the next few minutes.

The year they'd waited was finally over.

The time had been well spent, growing together in love and respect, counseling to put past wounds to rest once and for all. But now he was ready. And he thanked God Kyra was as anxious as he was to finally be his wife.

"I wish your mother were here today to see how beautiful you are."

Lace and tulle softly rustling, Kyra hugged her dad. He looked so handsome and dignified in his suit with his temples graying. And she felt like a fairy-tale princess in her long gown and flowing veil.

"Me, too, Dad. I miss her so much." Though something deep inside her believed her mother would be here, at least in spirit.

Amy, in drill-sergeant mode, swept past. "Time to start, y'all. Wade and the groomsmen are in place."

Kyra's stomach quivered.

She'd expected to be nervous. But she wasn't. Excited, yes, thrilled, absolutely, but calm and confident that God had ordained this marriage and that she and Wade were about to begin a wonderful life together.

She, Wade and their children.

"One minute." Careful not to step on her train, she crouched before the triplets. Ben and Caden were dressed identical to the groomsmen and Abby wore a long mint dress with a flower garland in her brown baby-fine hair.

Kyra's heart surged with love. They, like their dad, were a gift from God.

Adjusting the boys' ties and tucking their shirts for the third time, Kyra smooched each one on the cheek. Abby twirled in circles, fascinated with the swirl and swish of her chiffon skirt. Kyra caught her in mid spin for a hug.

Then her aunts, Patty and Hannah, funneled the adorable trio out the door to a grassy path strewn with flower petals.

Kyra tucked her hand into her father's elbow and stepped into place.

The hired keyboardist and his musical trio struck the opening notes of the "Bridal Chorus."

The triplets trotted down the nature-made aisle, waving small banners that proclaimed, Here comes the bride!

Soft chuckles and wide smiles greeted the babies.

As she began her walk, Kyra looked up. Her breath caught.

Her handsome groom waited beneath a rose-and-chiffon-draped arch, watching her with love in his eyes.

Behind him, a multicolored carpet of God's glory spread over the hills and valleys beneath a sky so blue she could almost taste it. Fluffy clouds drifted above the rounded mountaintops.

The outdoor setting could not have been more perfect. But even nature's glory was eclipsed by the way her heart yearned toward the man waiting to be her forever.

When they reached the arch, her father gently placed her hand into Wade's and stepped into his role as officiant.

Wade tucked her fingers into his strong rancher's hand. Where she wanted to be. Where she belonged.

"Marriage," her dad began after the welcome and prayer, "is more than a legal contract and the exchange of a few words. It is a sacred, eternal bond between a man and a woman. God, Who created us from the beginning of time as male and female for this very purpose said, 'Therefore shall a man leave his father and mother and shall cleave only unto his wife, and they shall be one flesh.'

"Deuteronomy 7:9 states, 'Know therefore that the Lord thy God, He is God, the faithful God, which keepeth covenant with them that love Him and keep His commandments to a thousand generations.'

"A covenant is permanent and must not be entered into lightly. After much prayer and study, Wade and Kyra come before us today to commit to a covenant marriage, an unbreakable, eternal relationship of spirit, soul and body."

With her dad's words in her head, Kyra glanced at Wade and saw the reflection of her deep commitment to him and their life together.

Today, they'd enter forever. She was ready.

Wade's blood thundered in his temples as he listened to the pastor. No words could adequately convey the love and commitment he wanted to give to Kyra. In a thousand years, he'd never be able to love her as much as she deserved.

But he'd live the rest of his life trying.

The pastor continued, taking them through the traditional ceremony. They exchanged rings, and Wade was proud to wear this symbol of his covenant with Kyra. He treasured each word Kyra spoke and refused to be embarrassed when emotion moistened his eyes and threaded his own promises.

Kyra was worth his emotion.

At last, it came time to share the words they'd written for each other.

Wade cleared his throat, holding fast to both of his Kyra's silky hands. "Kyra, my love, my beautiful bride, I am overwhelmingly grateful and proud to commit my life and that of my children to you. I am a better man, a better Christian and a better father because you're in my life. You loved me and my children even when I didn't believe in love. I didn't know what I needed, but God did.

And He sent you. So, I vow to love you as my own body, to cherish you even as the Lord cherishes the church and gave Himself for her. I promise to serve the Lord at your side and to be faithful to you every day of my life."

With trembling lips and teary eyes, Kyra received her groom's pledge. Then it was her turn.

"Wade, my love," she said, "God had a plan when He led me to the Sundown Ranch. I didn't understand it then. Now, I see. My body and mind needed to heal. Your heart needed mending. We needed each other, but God's plan was even better than simple need. He gave us love. He gave us family."

Thick emotion clogged her throat. She paused, fighting to continue.

Wade leaned close and whispered, "You're amazing."

Through tears, she smiled. "Is that supposed to help?"

They both laughed, as he'd known they would and, once composed, she continued.

"I choose you to be my forever. I commit to love you in word and action and to serve our Savior with you. I give you myself, all of me, and promise to be faithful, to respect and honor you and to proudly stand at your side as long as I live. With God as our guide, we'll weather any storms and come out stronger. I believe in you. I believe in us."

With hearts full, they lit a unity candle, and after the final words and prayer, the pastor said those lovely words. "I now pronounce you man and wife. Wade, son-in-law, you may kiss your bride."

Grinning, Wade leaned in to kiss his wife. Just then a commotion erupted on the front row. Laughter tittered through the guests.

In the front row, Benjamin broke loose from Aunt

Hannah and rushed to Wade, arms stretched high. "Daddy, Daddy! I kiss. I kiss."

Laughing with their guests, Wade lifted his son for Kyra's smooch.

She motioned for the other two. Even in her gorgeous gown, Kyra wouldn't ignore his kids. *Her* kids, too, a blessing he'd never dreamed possible.

Together, they crouched to receive their little family with kisses and hugs all around.

The musicians continued to play the recessional, so he took the hint and pulled Kyra to her feet.

A single scarlet cardinal fluttered past. Kyra followed the flight with her head.

"Wade, look."

He turned toward the mountains to see the bird circle and land on the unity table.

She'd told him about her love of cardinals, of the way their bright color outside her hospital window had cheered her, of how they reminded her of her mother.

For the rest of his life, when he saw a cardinal, Wade would think of this day, of the day God had given him the treasure of Kyra.

From reluctant nanny to loving mother and wife, his city girl was his now and he was hers.

And together they were the family they'd both always wanted.

* * * * *

Look for more books from
New York Times *bestselling author*
Linda Goodnight coming soon!

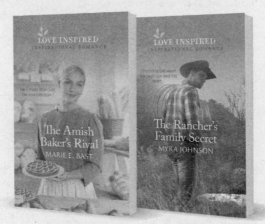